Shannon's Story

**Other books by
Ann M. Martin**

Rachel Parker, Kindergarten Show-off
Eleven Kids, One Summer
Ma and Pa Dracula
Yours Turly, Shirley
Ten Kids, No Pets
Slam Book
Just a Summer Romance
Missing Since Monday
With You and Without You
Me and Katie (the Pest)
Stage Fright
Inside Out
Bummer Summer

BABY-SITTERS LITTLE SISTER series
THE BABY-SITTERS CLUB mysteries
THE BABY-SITTERS CLUB series

Shannon's Story
Ann M. Martin

AN
APPLE
PAPERBACK

SCHOLASTIC INC.
New York Toronto London Auckland Sydney

ISBN 0-590-47756-0

Copyright © 1994 by Ann M. Martin. All rights reserved. Published by Scholastic Inc. THE BABY-SITTERS CLUB and APPLE PAPERBACKS are registered trademarks of Scholastic Inc.

12 11 10 9 8 7 6 5 4 3 2 1   4 5 6 7 8 9/9

Printed in the U.S.A.   40

First Scholastic printing, September 1994

The author gratefully acknowledges
Nola Thacker
for her help in
preparing this manuscript.

Shannon's Story

CHAPTER 1

"A sardine chocolate cake," I said.

My sister Maria made a gagging noise and went off into a storm of giggles. When she'd managed to get control of herself, she answered, "A broccoli milkshake with chopped onions."

"Euuuuuw," I said, grabbing my throat and making a face.

Maria began to giggle again.

We both looked at Tiffany. But she didn't seem to be listening. She just stared out the window as our school bus pulled to a stop in front of our house.

The three of us got out, Maria with a hop, Tiffany with her head down, and me last, with a wave to the driver. As the bus pulled away, I paused to look up and down our street. The day was bright and quiet and still, and you could feel spring just waiting to happen in Stoneybrook, where we live. My sisters Maria and Tiffany and I had been playing an old game of ours on the bus ride home from Stoneybrook Day School: Gross Food.

At least, Maria, who is eight, and I had been playing. Tiffany hadn't said anything at all.

I looked over at Tiffany as she walked beside me. Her head was still down and she was holding her backpack across her chest. Maybe now that she was eleven, Tiffany thought she was too old for the Gross Food game. Maybe she thought her older sister (that's me) shouldn't be playing it either. Maybe I'd embarrassed her and that's why she was ignoring us.

Or maybe she hadn't even noticed what Maria and I had been doing. It was hard to tell with Tiffany these days. She'd gotten very quiet lately, even quieter than usual.

"Marshmallow and spinach pie," said Maria.

I smiled. "Hmm," I said. "That doesn't sound so bad."

"Shannon!" shrieked Maria in delighted disgust.

"I'm raising spinach in my garden," said Tiffany softly.

I looked back at Tiffany in surprise. She had been listening after all.

"You are?" I said.

Tiffany nodded. She'd just started a garden in the very back corner of the backyard and

2

was spending hours there these days.

"Is it hard?" I asked.

"No. Spinach grows well in cool weather, like early spring and in the fall," answered Tiffany. After a moment, she added, "Broccoli, too. And cabbage. And peas."

Maria, bouncing happily on her toes, said, "I wish you could grow chocolate in your garden, Tiff."

Tiffany smiled, but she didn't answer.

"Maybe it's a good thing you can't," I said. "Chocolate is really bad for dogs, but they love it. Astrid would probably come out and eat any chocolate right up!"

"I'm glad *I'm* not a dog," Maria said. "I'd hate not to get to eat chocolate." She paused, then added thoughtfully, "I'm hungry."

"How about some nice pepper ice cream with garlic sauce?" I teased.

Maria kept her face straight with an effort. "I can't," she said as we pushed open the door of our house. "I have swim practice, thank you."

"We're home," I called.

Maria bounded off to her room to get her swimming gear. As silently as a fish in water, Tiffany slipped away. I had a feeling she would be changing out of her school uniform and into gardening clothes.

I headed for my room.

"Shannon?" My mother's voice came from the den.

I stopped and looked in. My mother was sitting on the couch holding a book. "Did you have a good day at school?"

"Same as always," I said.

"No new teachers? New friends? New news? What about your club meeting?"

"The Baby-sitters Club meets on Mondays, Wednesdays, and Fridays, Mom," I said. "Today is Thursday."

"Oh. Right." My mom nodded and smiled. I smiled back.

Some people think my mother and I look alike, but I think she and Tiffany look more alike. All three of us have thick, blonde hair and blue eyes and high cheekbones. But my mom and Tiffany wear their hair short and I wear mine long. And they both have these incredible dark eyelashes. I have to wear black mascara every day to make my eyelashes as dark as theirs. It's funny how families look alike in such mixed-up ways. My face is longer, shaped more like my father's. He's not very tall, and I'm not going to be really tall either, I can tell. But Mom is tall, and so is Tiffany and so is Maria. Maria, however, has the same dark coloring as my father and his brown eyes. If you looked at us altogether, though, you'd know we are related, that we're a family.

"An anchovy cheese slush!" cried Maria, skidding down the hall outside the den.

"Maria, slow down!" said my mother. Hearing my mother say that was funny, because she moves at hyper-speed a lot herself, just the way Maria does.

"Can't," said Maria breathlessly. "I've got to go to swim practice."

Just at that moment, a car horn sounded outside. "That's my ride!" exclaimed Maria.

"A peanut butter and ketchup sandwich," I called after Maria as she bolted for the door.

"Euuuuuw," she said. The door slammed behind her, cutting her off.

"The Gross Food game," said my mother. "How about — chocolate-grapefruit sundae?"

"I don't know, Mom. Sometimes I think chocolate goes with everything."

My mom laughed a little. "That's true. Well, then . . . a . . . a . . ."

I laughed a little, too. "I think Maria might be the family champion at this. I'd better go start on my homework."

"Shannon? I was thinking of taking Astrid for a walk. Do you want to come along?"

I stopped and turned around.

"I really have to get my homework done,"

I said. "Thanks anyway. I'll take Astrid later if you want."

My mother looked disappointed for a moment. Then she said, "Maybe Tiffany will want to go."

"Well, if she doesn't, I'll make it an extralong walk for Astrid," I promised. "As soon as I get the math out of the way."

"If you change your mind," my mother said.

"I'll let you know," I finished. I walked down the hall and up the stairs to my room.

Putting my books down on my desk, I looked out the window. Tiffany was already hard at work on her garden, with Astrid sitting nearby, watching attentively. Tiffany had changed out of the SDS uniform and was wearing faded jeans, sneakers, a big, grubby sweat shirt, and some old gloves that looked too large for her. Probably my father's, I thought. He'd been a serious gardener for awhile, back when I'd been just a kid, but he hadn't done anything outside in the yard for a long time except cook at a Fourth of July barbecue my parents had had last summer.

I smiled, remembering that: my father in his barbecue apron with a tall, silly chef's hat on his head, chasing Astrid, who had managed to grab two hot dogs off the end of the fork as he was lifting them from the grill onto a plate. He hadn't been able to catch her but it

6

had been a lot of fun. He and my mom had laughed and laughed and she'd told us the story of how she and Dad had cooked dinner for our grandparents, Dad's parents, when she and Dad had first gotten married, and Mom had dropped the pot roast in the middle of the kitchen.

"What did you do?" cried Tiffany.

My father had wriggled his eyebrows and said in a high voice like Julia Childs, "You're always alone in the kitchen."

"You ate it?" Maria had asked.

"We washed it first," said my mom and she and Dad had started laughing all over again.

The grill was in the garage now. I wondered if we'd have a cookout this Fourth of July.

As I watched, Tiffany knelt down, picked up a spade, and began to dig in her garden. She worked with slow, intense concentration. She was like my father that way.

Concentration. It was time I concentrated on my homework. I had a math test coming up the next week, and if I didn't study now, I'd have to work on it over the weekend. *That* was definitely not part of my game plan.

I pulled out my math book and sat down with a sigh.

I'm not crazy about math the way Maria is, but I do well in school and that's important to me. So I concentrated pretty intensely that afternoon. When I finally stood up to take a break over an hour had passed.

I looked out the window. Tiffany was still in the garden. She wasn't digging now. In fact, she wasn't doing much of anything. She looked as if she were just sitting there. And Astrid was still sitting next to her.

She *didn't* look as if she'd gone on a walk with Astrid and Mom. I decided that I had time to take Astrid for a good long walk before our father got home for dinner. Besides, I reasoned, if I did any more math, it was going to spoil my appetite.

Slamming the math book shut, I headed down to get Astrid's leash.

"Shannon?" My mother's disembodied voice came from the kitchen this time.

I felt a twinge of exasperation. Who else did my mom think it would be? "Yes?" I said, unhooking Astrid's leash from the back of the hall closet door.

"Where are you going?"

"Out to take Astrid for a walk," I said.

"Now?" said my mother. She came to the door, holding a stirring spoon in her hand.

"There's plenty of time before dinner," I said.

"It's your turn to set the table, you know," my mother reminded me.

"I know. I'll get it done."

"You don't want to keep me company while I finish up dinner?"

"Let me give Astrid that walk first," I said.

I closed the closet door and turned to see that my mother was frowning. "What is it, Mom?"

"You should wear a jacket," she said. "It's still kind of chilly out."

"This is a heavy sweater. It'll be plenty warm," I answered.

"You really should wear a jacket," my mother insisted.

"Mom! I don't need a jacket!" I heard how sharp my voice sounded and felt bad. But why wouldn't my mother listen to me? Why did she keep treating me as if I were eight years old, like Maria, instead of thirteen and old enough to know whether or not to wear a jacket?

I could tell my mother was about to say something else, and I braced myself, but the telephone came to the rescue with a shrill beep.

"I'll get it!" I said hastily and swooped down the hall and grabbed the receiver. "Hello?"

"Shanny?"

"Hi, Dad. How's it going?"

"I'm not going to be home for dinner.

Would you tell your mom for me?"

So what else is new, I wanted to say. Instead I said, "Okay."

"Work," said my father.

For a moment I thought he was talking about me, asking if I'd finished my homework. I almost told him that I had the math nailed down. But as he went on, I realized he wasn't talking about me at all.

"It's gonna drive me crazy. But what can I do?"

"Okay," I said again.

"Right. Well, I've got to go. See you guys later."

"Okay," I said for the third time. "Good-bye."

But my father had already hung up the phone. I put the receiver down slowly and walked back to the kitchen.

My mother was stirring something on the stove, staring off into space.

"Mom?"

She looked around. "Oh. Shannon. Phone for me?"

"It was Dad," I said.

"He won't be home for dinner, right?" asked my mom.

"Good guess," I said.

She smiled, a little smile that didn't reach her eyes. "I suppose it's some trial, as usual."

My father's a lawyer with a big firm. He works a lot. And lately, he had missed a lot of family dinners. Even more than usual. Some case he'd been working on for a long time was just coming up for trial, a big case that had even been written up in the newspaper.

He barely had time for his Rotary club meetings and board meetings and jogging and lunches and dinners with clients.

Or for dinner at home. Sometimes, he wasn't even home by the time I went to sleep.

I remembered the Fourth of July barbecue again and felt a sudden surge of disappointment. I'd wanted my father to be home for dinner. I'd wanted to sit around the table with my family and talk to them. I'd wanted to listen to my mother and father tell jokes and stories and ask Tiffany how her garden was growing and Maria if going to swim practice every day was turning her hair green.

But I guessed it wasn't going to happen that night.

"I'll go walk Astrid," I said.

My mother didn't mention the jacket again. She just said, "Don't stay out too long. Maria will be home from swim practice soon and it'll be time for dinner."

"I'll set the table as soon as I get back," I offered.

"Fine," said my mother, turning back to the stove.

I called Astrid in from the backyard, waving the leash. Astrid came racing to me with an undignified, doggy grin, wriggling with delight at the prospect of a walk.

"I'm taking Astrid for a walk," I called to Tiffany. "Want to come?"

But Tiffany, who'd turned when I'd called, was already turning back as she shook her head no. As we left the house, I looked over the fence. Tiffany was still in her garden at the foot of the yard. I could see my mother at the kitchen window on the side of the house, moving slowly back and forth, her head down. My father was still at work. Maria was still at swim practice.

It made me feel weird. Like my family was a bunch of those magnetized marbles that roll around all over the place and sometimes come together and stick and sometimes repel each other like they don't belong together at all. It was as if we were all in the "marble-repel" mode. We might look alike, we might look as if we belong to the same family.

But right now, we didn't feel like it. I felt weird. And sort of sad, somehow.

CHAPTER 2

"Big day today at school?" asked my mother.

I gulped down my orange juice and said, "Well, uh . . ."

Tiffany didn't say anything. Dad didn't say anything either because he had already left for his office.

Maria said, "We've got a *killer* practice this afternoon."

"You have swim practice this afternoon, too?"

Maria looked at Mom in surprise. "Of course," she said.

"The bus is here," I said and we made a break for the door.

"Shannon?"

"Uh, yeah, Mom?"

"You'll be home this afternoon, of course."

"French Club meeting, then Baby-sitters Club," I said. " 'Bye. . . ."

I hurried out of the house before Mom could ask me any more questions. She *knew* I had BSC meetings every Monday, Wednesday, and Friday. Why didn't she ever listen? Plus I hated when the bus driver sat there with the door open, waiting, while everybody watched from the windows as I ran toward the bus. Maria might like sports, but beyond soccer at school, which I happen to like a lot, I'm not into running or moving fast. I like to do things at my own speed, my own way. It is one of the things that makes me a good student — that and the fact that I like school.

It's true. In spite of having to wear uniforms (we all do at Stoneybrook Day School, from kindergarten right on up) and having major amounts of homework and a lot more rules than, say, Stoneybrook Academy, or Stoneybrook Middle School, I like learning things. And I like having teachers who know the things I want to learn.

In spite of how conservative it is, SDS is pretty good about letting you take interesting courses. For instance, this year, I was taking advanced French, accelerated math, and philosophy, I was playing soccer for my gym credit, and I was taking an astronomy unit as part of my science requirement — an astronomy unit that I had set up with four other kids. Sometimes, if you are interested in a subject, SDS will even let you set up a unit for credit, a unit you study with just the teacher, like an independent study in college. But then, at SDS, you're expected to go to college.

SDS even looks a little bit like a college campus. It's made up of four redbrick buildings set around a grass courtyard and connected to each other and to the administration office in the front by covered walkways. The offices are in an old house (the land for the school was donated by the woman who used to live in the house), and the gym and the track and playing fields are in the back. Of course, the fact that all of the students are wearing uniforms lets you know right away that we aren't really on a college campus, even if seeing all the little kids in kindergarten didn't give it away.

Another decent thing about SDS is that I'm not the only one who likes school. Most of my friends there do, too. We all have favorite subjects and it's cool to talk about something you're studying if it really interests you. Right now, I'm the "ask the astronomy student" at my table at lunch.

But our current favorite topic is French. *Mais oui.*

That means, literally, "but yes" in French. I guess a loose translation would be "of course!"

Mais oui we love French? You better believe it. Because our advanced eighth grade French class is going on a class trip to Paris for *one whole week* when school is out at the end of May — everyone, that is, with a B average overall and an 85 average in French.

Madame DuBarry announced the trip the first week of school this semester, and we've been practicing our French like mad ever since, so we'll be *très, très bon*. (Very, very good.)

"Good morning, Ms. Kilbourne." That was Dr. Patek. She's the headmistress of SDS. Her office is in the administration house, but she makes a point of being around the buildings when classes are starting for the day. She also makes a point of knowing all our names.

"*Bonjour*, Dr. Patek," I said.

Maria and Tiffany had peeled off in search of their own friends the moment we'd gotten off the bus, so Dr. Patek didn't say hello to any more Kilbournes. But if she had, she wouldn't have called them Ms. Kilbourne. They would have been Maria and Tiffany. It's not until middle school that Dr. Patek "promotes" you.

Cool. I mean, *très bon*.

Just then I saw my best friend at SDS. "Uh, 'bye, Dr. Patek," I said.

"*A bientôt,*" said Dr. Patek.

Grinning, I hurried over to Greer Carson. Greer often rides the bus, but not always. Sometimes she gets a ride with her older brother.

"Hey!" I said. "Did you finish your math? I was going to call you last night, but I didn't realize until I was already in bed that I wasn't sure about one of the problems after all."

Greer shook her head so that her long, red-brown curly hair, cut at a severe blunt angle from front to back, swept her shoulders. Like Claudia and Stacey in the BSC, Greer is serious about fashion, and she doesn't let the fact that we have to wear uniforms cramp her style.

Greer also has a *big* dramatic streak. After shaking her head, she ran her hands through her hair on either side of her face and pressed the heels of her palms against her temples, rolling her eyes up. She looked like a mad scientist. "I *hate* that," she cried. "I just *hate it* when that happens."

"Yeah, I couldn't sleep all night, Greer," I said.

Greer wrote me off as a sympathetic audience, dropped her hands, and grabbed her pack, turning briskly practical. "So, which problem was it?"

We had our heads bent over the problem, arguing, when Margaret Jardin came up. Margaret usually rides the bus, but sometimes she walks. If you think Margaret's last name sounds French, you are right (It means "garden."). She even has a great-aunt and some relatives still living in France. But we don't call her Margaret, we call her Meg. Meg's good at French, but she's not really excited about it. What excites Meg is astronomy. In fact, she's one of the people in my astronomy unit.

"Guess what?" she said. "There's going to be a meteor shower this weekend. Maybe we can all stay over at my house and watch it."

"Cool," I said. "We can also start studying for finals."

Meg and Greer both made faces. I laughed. "Okay, we'll start *worrying* about finals, then."

"You worry," retorted Meg. "I'm worried about our project for French class. Plan a menu for a meal? In French? I mean, if I wanted to take home economics, I'd take it."

"We don't have home economics at SDS, Meg," Greer pointed out.

Meg shrugged. "Whatever."

"You don't have to plan a *balanced* menu," I said. "You can put anything on it. You just have to get the French right."

Meg thought about that for a moment, then said thoughtfully, *"Pommes frites?"*

"French fries is a start," I said. "It's on *my* menu."

Just then the first bell rang. We joined the other students drifting slowly up the shallow stairs into the building.

"I guess it could come in handy," Meg said as we walked into our homeroom. "I mean, when we get to Paris. I'd hate not to know how to order fries! Now all I have to do is learn how to say, 'extra large, with ketchup' in French!"

Do you get the idea that we are all excited about the BCT (Big Class Trip?). You're right. We are. Wildly, uncoolly, totally revved. We've been watching French movies or anything that has anything French in it (we're on the track of an old movie called *Sabrina* with Audrey Hepburn, who goes to France), trying to speak French, even buying French fashion magazines. No chance any of us are not going to keep our overall B averages in school, or make anything less than an 85 in French. Because if we do, it's no go.

Très simple.

I handed in my math homework feeling good about working out that problem and knowing that it was a perfect paper. I like math. And math is a universal language, did you know that? Mathematicians from different countries can meet and even if they don't speak each other's language, they can write math problems in mathematical symbols and understand each other.

So in a way, I was studying more languages than just French. I mean, I was taking English, too; and astronomy is sort of the language of the galaxies, right?

Okay, okay, I'm getting all soppy, but you see what I mean?

Anyway, I was pleased with the thought. I was toying with it in my head as an idea for an English essay when Madame DuBarry's voice interrupted me.

"Mademoiselle?"

I jumped about a mile. "Uh — *oui*, Madame?"

Madame smiled. She is a tall, energetic woman, who always wears bright colors and the same diamond earrings every day. The diamonds are beautiful. I found myself staring at them now, as if they'd give me an answer.

"Mademoiselle, we were talking about holding another fund-raiser for our trip to Paris. Any ideas?"

"*Non*, Madame."

Madame let me off the hook, merely nodding and moving on to the next person. Whew. Madame could be really bad — *très mal*, I think — about paying attention and participating in class. It was part of our grade.

Not that I was worried. My average in French was one of my highest in any subject. And I always keep up with my schoolwork in every subject. During exams I set up a study schedule for myself and stick to it. It's easier, actually, than worrying about studying.

But I didn't want to take chances. I didn't want *anything* to come between me and Paris.

CHAPTER 3

"Shanny?"

I made a face at my mom's use of my baby name and continued yanking off my school uniform and getting into decent clothes — jeans, a big cotton sweater, loafers. I'd stayed after school for a meeting of the French club, practicing conversational French and giggling (I hope giggling is a universal language!), and I was going to be late for my BSC meeting if I didn't majorly step on it.

"Shanny?"

I hopped to the door of my room, pulling on a sock.

"Yo, Mom, I'm late, okay?" I called. "I have a BSC meeting."

"Yo?" said my mother, sounding disapproving. "Where do you *learn* this slang?"

"It just means . . . never mind. Anyway, I'm off to the BSC."

"Again?" said Mom.

I felt a momentary stab of annoyance. Hadn't I told Mom that this very morning? And why did she sound so critical, as if my meeting was some weird indulgence of base desires? I mean, it's a business and I work hard at it, even if I do have a lot of fun.

I also felt a little guilty, which I hated. My mom's voice sounded almost hurt.

But that wasn't my fault, was it?

I found my loafers, pulled one on, hopped back to the top of the stairs, and sat down to pull it on. "Again," I mimicked my mom's query, trying to keep my voice light (not easy to do when you're shouting down the stairs).

Mom appeared at the bottom of the stairs.

"Maria's at swim practice," she said. (This I knew. Maria is always at swim practice. And besides, she'd already told us she would be there this morning.)

I nodded and pulled on my other shoe. "Tiff's out in her garden," I said as neutrally as I could.

My mom smiled a little. "My grandmother used to garden. But I never did like it very much. You have to wait so *long* for the flowers to come up after you put the seeds in."

I laughed and shook my head. "You're into instant gratification? I didn't know adults were allowed to do that!"

My mom didn't laugh. In fact, she looked

kind of sad. "I don't know what I'm into," she said after a moment. Then, quickly, "Listen, Shannon, why don't you have your meeting over here? I could make some cookies and . . ."

"We always have it at Claudia's because Claudia has her own phone. Our clients all call us at that number. They expect us to be there, Mom." I tried not to sound impatient, but I *knew* my mom knew this.

"Oh." A one-two punch. She sounded both disapproving *and* disappointed.

"Tiffany's garden looked pretty good from the bedroom window, Mom," I went on. "You ought to go check it out." Wow, who did I sound like? In fact, what did this whole conversation remind me of? Well, I didn't have time to think about it just then. I stood up and bounded down the stairs.

"Gotta go," I said and shot past Mom and out the door before she could make any more suggestions. Kristy Thomas, the founder and president of the BSC, is a real stickler for punctuality. She lives across the street from me, and her brother Charlie drives her to meetings. Today he was giving me a ride, too.

Kristy must have been hovering by the front door, because it opened before I even dashed up the steps. "We're ready, Charlie!" she called back into the house without even saying hello.

That was cool. I was used to Kristy's ways now. When we'd first met, we hadn't liked each other at all. Kristy was new to the neighborhood and she thought I was an awful snob, and I thought she was a jerk who was stealing all my baby-sitting jobs. But we'd gotten past that and Kristy had even invited me to join the BSC as an associate member, to help out when other members couldn't take babysitting jobs. Now, with the BSC's regular member, alternate officer Dawn Schafer, making a long visit to her father and younger brother on the Coast (the West Coast, as in California), I was attending a lot more meetings. And doing a lot more baby-sitting. I didn't mind, though. Not only were the meetings fun and the work, too (mostly), but I was saving every penny for my trip to Paris.

"Punctuality is the courtesy of kings," announced Kristy as Charlie slid into the car, where Kristy had already hustled me. She was talking to Charlie but I knew her comment was also aimed at me. I hid a smile. King Kristy? With Kristy, it just might happen.

"Hey, they're not going to start without the *president*, are they?" Charlie teased.

Kristy looked stern for a moment longer,

then her face relaxed into a grin. "They'll start on Claudia's stash of treats without me," she said.

"That's for sure," I agreed and we gave each other a knowing look.

Claudia Kishi, artist and maverick student, is a secret reader of Nancy Drew books. Hidden around her room at any given moment you are likely to find at least half a dozen Nancy Drews. (Claudia's parents just don't understand why Claudia won't read more "serious" books, the way her older sister Janine does. Janine's a high school student who is a genuine genius. She even takes college courses because she's advanced beyond what the high school can teach her in some subjects.)

Guess what. Claudia is also a world-class junk food addict. A collector's cache of junk food is part of Claudia's hidden decor. You think I'm kidding? You haven't watched Claudia reach down behind an open drawer and produce chocolate-covered coffee beans, or slide her hand between her mattress and box springs and pull out chocolate-covered Oreos and half a box of graham crackers.

We rode the rest of the way to Claudia's comparing Claudia Kishi junk food notes (Charlie couldn't believe it!) and we got there with three minutes to spare.

Janine let us in.

"Merci," I said airily as we charged up the stairs to Claudia's room.

"Bon après-midi," replied Janine, wishing us good afternoon in French without missing a beat. A genius, see what I mean?

Claudia was just passing around a package of Mallomars and a package of oatmeal raisin Frookies. Mallomars are a big club favorite and I knew they'd be gone before the meeting was over. The Frookies, which are special healthy cookies made without sugar, would last a little longer.

The Frookies are for Stacey McGill, mainly, and Dawn (when she's here). You'll hear more about them and everyone in the BSC later, but first I should tell you how the club works.

The BSC was an inspired idea from the churning, seething brain of our fearless leader, Kristy. It came to her one night when she was at home, listening to her mother call baby-sitter after baby-sitter for her little brother, David Michael. That's when it hit Kristy: why not call one number and be able to reach several sitters at once?

In what seemed like no time at all, the BSC was set up, meeting Monday, Wednesday, and Friday afternoons at Claudia's from 5:30 until 6:00. That's when clients call to set up baby-sitting jobs. The three original members of the BSC, Kristy, Claudia (BSC vice-president who lived across the street from her), and Mary Anne (BSC secretary who lived next door to Kristy and had been Kristy's best friend *forever*), weren't sure three people were enough for a club. So they invited Stacey McGill, who was new in town and becoming friends with Claudia, to join. She became the treasurer. Then Dawn Schafer followed, to become the alternate officer. That means she takes over the duties of anyone who can't make a meeting. Then came Jessica Ramsey and Mallory Pike as junior officers. Now there is one other associate member, too: Logan Bruno (who is also Mary Anne's boyfriend). Associate members don't have to attend meetings, but they can, and they also take any jobs that won't fit into the BSC schedule.

Kristy not only thought up the BSC, she also added other Kristy touches — like the record book, the notebook, and Kid-Kits.

The record book is where we keep all our appointments. Plus a list of clients and any special information about them, *plus* a record of our dues and expenses. The record book is the secretary's responsibility, except for the money part, which is the treasurer's.

We all use the notebook. We have to write about every job in it *and* read each other's entries. It helps us keep up with what's going on in regular clients' lives (like who's teething or who's developed a new passion for dogs, for example). It also helps us learn how to deal with new problems that come up — we learn from what others write down.

Kid-Kits? They are boxes we've all fixed up with puzzles, games, toys, books, colored pencils, stamps, stickers, and all kinds of fun things. Some of it is our old stuff. Some of it we buy out of BSC funds. We take the kits on some jobs and the kids *love* them. Even though some of the toys and books are old, they're new to the kids. And, as Kristy noticed, kids *always* love to play with other kids' toys!

So. Back to the members of the BSC.

I settled down on the floor with a couple of Mallomars and looked at Stacey as she took a Frookie out of the box, offered them to everyone else, and then put them down on the floor next to her.

Stacey, who as you now know is the BSC treasurer, is a math whiz. She is also diabetic. That means that she has to watch what she eats very carefully (no sugar! yuck) and even give herself shots or else she could get very, very sick. But Stacey is cool about it. In fact, she may be one of the coolest people I know, generally. For one thing, she is from New York City, which makes her just a little more sophisticated than most the kids her age around

Stoneybrook. She is tall and thin and has long blonde hair and is a way cool — no, make that *très* cool — dresser. (When you have to wear a uniform to school every day you *particularly* notice these things.)

Stacey lives with her mother. She came to Stoneybrook with her mother and her father, but then they got divorced after her family moved back to New York City. So Stacey returned to Stoneybrook with her mother (and are we ever glad she did.) Now Stacey visits her father in New York, which makes her bi-city (we tease Dawn about being bi-coastal because she has a family on both coasts) and keeps us posted on all the important cool things she thinks we need to know.

Given Stacey's style, it's not surprising that Claudia is her best friend. As I said earlier, Claud is an artist, with her own unique vision of the world (a vision that does not include liking school or being an honor role student!) and of the clothes she wears. For example, today Stacey looked ultra-city in black: black leggings, a black sweater, a big black belt with an oversized buckle, black Doc Martens, and her hair pulled back with a black and gold scarf that picked up the gold of the gold chain earrings she was wearing.

Claudia was beyond the city, maybe into outer space and looking outrageous, artistically terrific: an enormous pair of pants held up with a man's belt and a pair of neon purple suspenders, an enormous purple T-shirt over a tie-dyed long-underwear top, her long black hair pulled back into a braid clipped at intervals with little-kid barrettes, and these dangly peace-sign earrings.

Claudia always looks incredibly beautiful in anything she wears. In fact, she's probably the only person I know who could wear some of the clothes she wears!

Mary Anne is the opposite of Claudia and Stacey, style-wise and sophistication-wise. Until recently, Mary Anne was an only child, raised by her very caring but very strict father. It's not that Mr. Spier was an ogre, it's just that, as a single parent (Mary Anne's mother died when Mary Anne was just a baby) he didn't want to make any mistakes. Mary Anne had to work pretty hard to convince him she was growing up and could choose her own clothes and not wear her hair in little-kid pigtails. But although Mary Anne is one of the shyest and most sensitive, tender-hearted people in the known universe, she is also one of the strongest underneath. She toughed it out, and not only changed her wardrobe to something a little more typical Stoneybrook Middle School, she acquired a kitten, Tigger, and a boyfriend, Logan Bruno.

And then she acquired a whole new family, with the help of Dawn Schafer.

This is how it happened:

Dawn's mother grew up in Stoneybrook, moved away, and eventually got married. When she and Dawn's father got divorced, Mrs. Schafer moved back to Stoneybrook with Dawn and her younger brother Jeff. When Dawn and Mary Anne discovered that Mr. Spier and Mrs. Schafer were high school sweethearts, they did some matchmaking, and now Dawn and Mary Anne are sisters as well as friends. The new combined Schafer-Spier family lives in an old farmhouse (that might even be haunted), although Jeff eventually decided to move back to California and stay with his dad. Now Dawn is out in California visiting them for awhile.

Dawn is the third blonde in the BSC, except she has pale, pale long blonde hair. She's a casual dresser, and wears two earrings in each ear. She's very much into ecology and saving the earth, and she eats no red meat and hardly any sugar or junk food. That's why, if Dawn had been at the meeting, she'd be sharing the Frookies with Stacey. Like Mary Anne, Dawn has deep-rooted, strong, and sometimes stubborn feelings (about things such as the environment). But unlike Mary Anne, Dawn is quick to say what's on her mind, although not in a negative way. Overall, she's pretty easy-going, which makes her a good baby-sitter — and a good alternate officer.

Jessica Ramsey and Mallory Pike are eleven and in sixth grade and are younger than the rest of us (we're all thirteen and in eighth grade). As junior officers, they can't baby-sit at night (unless it's for their own families), just afternoons and weekend days.

Like Kristy and Mary Anne (and Mary Anne and Dawn), and Stacey and Claudia, they are best friends. Mallory comes from a *huge* family. She has four brothers (three of them are triplets) and three sisters. Needless to say, the Pike family calls on the BSC quite a bit. In fact, that's how the BSC members first met Mallory, who was one of the baby-sittees. But when the club needed more members, it seemed natural to turn to Mallory.

Mallory has red hair, and wears braces and glasses (although she is campaigning *hard* for contact lenses). She loves to read, especially horse stories, and she wants to be a children's book writer and illustrator when she grows up.

Jessica Ramsey, on the other hand, is planning on being a prima ballerina. She's already danced (even starred) in some productions and she takes special dancing lessons. Jessi comes from a much smaller family than Mallory, and has only two siblings — an eight-year-old sister and a baby brother. She shares Mallory's love of reading and of horses, especially any horse story by Marguerite Henry.

Like Dawn and Stacey, Jessi and her family recently moved to Stoneybrook. Jessi had some of the same moving-to-a-new-town problems that Dawn and Stacey did, plus one. Because Jessi is black, she came up against some ignorance — in the form of prejudice. It took awhile for people to settle down and learn just how stupid their prejudices were, but they finally did.

Our other associate member is Logan Bruno (who usually doesn't come to meetings). As a guy, Logan can bring some special skills to his BSC jobs, and has. And as Mary Anne's boyfriend as well as a BSC member, he can always be counted on to help out. He moved to Stoneybrook from Kentucky and has a soft Southern drawl and easygoing ways. Mary Anne thinks he looks just like her favorite star, Cam Geary. I have to admit, Logan *is* major cute.

And that's the BSC, except for one other VIM (Very Important Member), President Kristy Thomas. Kristy is the shortest member of the BSC, as well as one of the shortest people in her whole class at school. She's a way casual dresser (new jeans and recently washed sneakers are her idea of dressing up), and she's one of the few people I know who's busier than I am. She even coaches a softball team made up of little kids, called Kristy's Krushers.

Kristy is also the other BSC member with a large family. She has three brothers — her younger brother David Michael, and her older brothers Charlie and Sam. She's also got a stepfather, Watson Brewer, who is a real, live millionaire and a fanatic gardener. Watson met Kristy's mother awhile ago and they fell in love (Kristy's father left when David Michael was just a baby and they hardly ever hear from him). Not much later, Mr. Brewer and Mrs. Thomas got married. So Kristy and her family moved from the house next to Mary Anne (where they'd been bursting at the seams) to Watson's mansion, which is across the street from our house. That's how Kristy and I met.

Anyway, now Kristy also has a younger stepsister and stepbrother, Karen and Andrew Brewer, who spend every other month with them, plus a little adopted sister, Emily Michelle, who is Vietnamese. And when Emily came, so did Kristy's grandmother, Nannie, to help take care of Emily and all the other things that were happening around the Thomas-Brewer mansion. And I shouldn't forget my god-dog, Shannon. She's named after me because I gave Kristy one of Astrid's puppies after their wonderful collie Louie died (in fact that's how Kristy and I really started becoming friends). There is also a fat, cranky cat named Boo-Boo, two goldfish, Karen's rat, Andrew's hermit crab, and an alleged ghost in the attic.

With all that going on, you can see why Kristy has to be super-organized and super-efficient!

Which is what she was being right now. She finished off her Mallomar in three quick (but efficiently chewed) bites, cleared her throat, and said, "Any new business?"

Everyone slowly shook their heads and we kept on with the business at hand — munching on the junk food.

"Well," said Kristy briskly, "has anybody happened to notice that Mother's Day is coming up?"

"Whoa, that's right!" Claudia slapped her palm to her forehead. "It's a good thing you reminded us, Kristy. I was about to use my last dollar on art supplies, and then I wouldn't have been able to get my mom anything decent for Mother's Day."

Mother's Day, I thought. Hmmm.

"Great, Claud, but I also brought it up for another reason. I think we should plan something special like we did before."

"Another Mother's Day surprise," said Mary Anne, clasping her hands.

As if on cue, the phone rang. Kristy picked it up. "Baby-sitters Club. How may I help you?"

She took down the information (one of our regular clients was calling, Mrs. Papadakis, who lives across the street from Kristy and next door to me) and told her she'd call right back. Then Mary Anne looked up our schedules in the BSC record book (in which she has never, ever made a mistake).

"Everyone is free except me," she reported. "But it's a Friday night baby-sitting job, so that lets you and Mal out, Jessi."

"Someday," said Jessi.

Mal made a face.

We all looked at each other. Then Stacey said, "Why don't you take it, Shannon? It's in your neighborhood."

"True," said Kristy. "And I've got Krushers practice the next morning. I wouldn't mind having Friday night free."

"Go for it," said Claudia. "You need the money for Paris, *oui*?"

I looked at Claudia in surprise. "You take French?" I asked.

"*Hai*," answered Claudia. "That's Japanese for yes. I also know the Spanish for yes. *Sí*."

She shrugged. "Call me multilingual."

"Wow, three languages," teased Stacey. "Say something else."

Claudia rolled her eyes and grinned. "I can understand some Japanese because my grandmother Mimi often spoke it. But I can't really speak it. When it comes to Spanish and French, *sí* and *oui* about does it."

"No, it doesn't, Claud. Think of all the great food words in French," I said.

Claud looked puzzled, then said, "French fries?"

We started laughing, and Mary Anne wrote my name into the schedule for the Papadakises and called Mrs. Papadakis back to tell her.

"Pommes frites," I said to Claudia as Kristy was hanging up. "That's French fries. At least, I think it is."

"You better make sure before you get to Paris," Claudia warned me solemnly.

"About Mother's Day," Kristy said loudly.

Quickly, we turned our attention back to our fearless leader. "So, here's the deal. We once gave the parents of the kids we sit for a special free day off on Mother's Day. Let's do something like that."

"Like that, but different," suggested Mary Anne. She'd had kind of a tough time last Mother's Day, but had finally solved her dilemma by getting her father a Mother's Day gift. That was before he and Mrs. Schafer got married. I wondered what she was going to do now.

"I'll have to get two Mother's Day presents," said Mary Anne.

That answered *that* question. But it didn't answer another question. What was *I* going to do about Mother's Day?

Kristy was going on, "So let's start thinking of ideas. We can discuss it at the next meeting, and then implement whatever plan we decide on."

I hid a grin at Kristy's official-sounding language. Besides, however Kristy said it, I knew that, as with all of Kristy's ideas, we'd be going full steam ahead in no time.

The phone rang again and we were kept pretty busy for the last few minutes of the meeting. In fact, we ended up staying a few minutes late and Kristy hustled me out the door after she'd adjourned the BSC meeting. We'd talked a little more about the Mother's Day surprise, but nothing concrete had come of it.

I had figured out one thing though. The funny feeling I'd had as I was leaving my house, when I'd teased Mom about instant gratification and tried to find her something to do, such as gardening with Tiffany, had reminded me of just what I did when I was baby-sitting: keeping the kids busy and happy.

Being around my mom these days made me feel as if I were the adult and she was the kid. And the unhappy kid, at that.

Things hadn't been great around our house, true. The last few holidays had been tense and pretty perfunctory. We'd have cake on birthdays, blow out the candles, and then all disappear, for example. And sometimes, my father would arrive so late that he might as well not have shown up at all.

None of us were happy with the way things were, I guess. But how had I ended up feeling responsible for my mom?

I didn't know, but I didn't like it.

And that was why I wasn't excited to be thinking about Mother's Day surprises or Mother's Day gifts or Mother's Day anything at all.

CHAPTER 4

Saturday morning. Hah. It was mine, mine, mine, all mine and I loved the *deeply* serious decision I faced when I first woke up: go back to sleep, or get up and do nothing.

Guilt-free either way.

The sound of my father's car backing out of the garage is what woke me. I rolled over and squinted at the dial of my Dream Machine. Wow. I'd have to remember this if I ever considered being a lawyer. Getting up at that hour is for early birds and worms.

And possibly Kristy, I thought sleepily.

I wondered if our fearless leader across the street was waking up early. If she was, I wondered if she'd face the same decision I'd make, or just get up automatically and start on some project. I decided that she'd do the project thing. Kristy is so organized that even her free time is organized.

On the other hand, I feel that free time is a

reward I earn for being so organized: true free time, when you don't have to be anywhere or do anything and your tests are studied for and your homework is under control and your chores are done.

Giving one last, brief thought to Kristy and what she might suggest I do with this vast, unbroken stretch of Saturday morning free time, I yawned. Then I made my decision: I rolled over and went back to sleep.

When I awoke again, it was past ten. The house was still quiet, but it was a different kind of quiet, an empty quiet.

I can be a morning person when I have to be, but when I don't have to be, I am a basic slug. I got up (slowly) and wandered around my room, thinking vaguely of breakfast and lunch and whether I had to get dressed. As I wandered by my bedroom window, a movement caught my eye and I realized that Tiffany was hard at work in her garden. I wondered how long she had been there and how much work anyone could possibly do in a garden, or at least in a garden the size of Tiffany's. It wasn't all that big.

Hmmm.

I pulled some jeans on, stuffed the shirt tail of my giant sleeping shirt into them, and wandered downstairs in search of breakfast. A note on the refrigerator door informed me that

Mom had taken Maria to a swim meet. All accounted for, if not present.

Breakfast was peaceful. I toasted English muffins and got all the flavors of jam out of the refrigerator and mixed them together in different combinations on my plate. It was something I used to do when I was a kid (okay, okay, so I was playing with my food like a little kid), but no one was around and it *was* Saturday morning. Then I reheated a cup of coffee in the microwave with half a cup of milk and three teaspoons of sugar.

Café au lait. Coffee with milk. That's what it's called. I wasn't sure how to say sugar. *Sucre?* But it was fun to imagine I was sitting in a Paris cafe with my friends, drinking coffee.

I made another cup of *café au lait* (mostly *au lait*) and headed out to the garden.

"Hi," I said. "How does your garden grow?"

Tiffany sat back on her heels and looked up at me with glowing eyes. "Look! The peas are coming up, just like it said in the book," she said. She pointed to a row of tiny pale green bean-sprout-looking things, just breaking the soil. Or I guess I mean pea sprouts.

"That's great, Tiffany," I said. "How long before we have peas?"

"This kind will make peas in forty days, this kind in forty-eight days," Tiffany said. "And

I put another row of the same in over there a week later so we'll have a long pea season. I love fresh peas, don't you?"

"Uh, yeah," I said.

"They're very sweet," said Tiffany. "This kind is called sugar snap. You can eat the peas and the pod!"

I wondered if Claudia had heard of sugar snap peas, and how they would rate on her junk food chart.

"You're turning into quite a gardener," I said. "Mom said her grandmother used to like to garden and had a real green thumb."

"Our great-grandmother? Maybe I inherited it from her," said Tiffany, looking even more pleased.

"Didn't Mom tell you that when you started working on your garden?"

Tiffany shook her head. "She just told me to be careful not to dig up the roses. As if I couldn't *see* a bunch of big, thorny rosebushes! Sometimes Mom treats me like a little kid."

"Yeah, I know what you mean," I said.

Picking up her trowel, Tiffany said invitingly, "You want to help? I'm digging manure in for tomato plants. Tomatoes are heavy feeders and need lots of nourishment."

"Manure? Um, no thanks," I said. "Maybe some other time."

"Okay." Tiffany went back to her gardening. As I left, I heard her begin to whistle tunelessly.

The sun felt good on my face. I sat on the back step while I finished my coffee and watched Tiffany work. Rule #2 about free time (right after rule #1, Do Nothing) is that free time feels even better if you are doing nothing and watching someone else work. Rule #2A is that the work has to be work you don't feel guilty about not doing yourself or helping to do.

I enjoyed rules #1-2A until the sun was high overhead and I heard Mom's car pull into the driveway. I got up and went into the kitchen and began to rinse my cup and breakfast things to put into the dishwasher.

"How'd it go?" I called.

"Maria's team won," said my mother's voice and a moment later she appeared in the kitchen door.

"Another victory for SDS Junior Swim Team," I said. "Where's Maria? I want to hear a splash-by-splash."

"Maria's freestyle relay came in third in one of the events," said my mother. "She and her teammates decided to stay after the meet and get some extra practice in. Something about faster starts."

"Oh," was all I could think of to say.

"Anybody call?" asked Mom.

Was she thinking about my father? I shook my head. It was hard to read my mother's expression.

"What about some lunch?" she said. "Watching all that swimming made me hungry."

"I've been goofing off all morning," I confessed. "And I'm hungry, too."

We made sandwiches and salads and Mom went out to get Tiffany. A few minutes later she returned, looking puzzled.

"Tiffany said she can't leave her garden right now."

"Won't," I said. "She's really into it."

Mom smiled. "She is, isn't she? It's nice to be so involved in something."

I wondered if Tiff wasn't getting a little too involved in her garden, but I didn't say anything. Instead, I poured out some seltzer and lime for Mom and some cola for me.

We ate in silence for a little while. Then Mom said, "Have some salad, Shannon. It's good for you."

"I don't want any, thanks," I said.

"Why don't you like salad?"

"I do like salad," I said, beginning to feel annoyed. "But I don't want any right now. I had breakfast just a little while ago."

"It's important for a growing girl to get

her vitamins," Mom said. She picked up the salad bowl and scooped some salad out onto my plate. "And you shouldn't have slept so late."

"Hey," I protested, stung by the criticism. "It's *my* free time. I work hard and I earned it and I can spend it sleeping late if I want to!"

"And *I* don't work hard?" retorted my mom, her lips getting thin.

"I didn't say that," I answered.

"Eat your salad." Maybe ordering me around was Mom's idea of hard work.

"No, *thank* you," I said, shoving the salad to one side with my fork. I must have pushed it a little more energetically than I meant to, because some of the salad fell off the plate and scattered on the table.

"Shannon!" said my mother.

"It's not my fault!" I could hear the whine in my voice and I began to get really steamed. I couldn't believe it. She was treating me like a child and I was starting to act like one, which made me even angrier. At least I didn't say, "You started it."

"Fine," snapped my mother. "Don't eat your salad."

"I won't," I snapped back.

We finished lunch in angry silence.

I cleared off the table (rattling the dishes

more than I needed to, I confess) and my mother picked up her purse from the table by the door.

"I've got some errands to do," she said. "Do we need anything from the grocery store?"

"Salad dressing," I said before I could stop myself.

My mother's lips tightened, but she didn't say anything. She just left.

And left me feeling like a jerk.

What had just happened? I couldn't figure it out. The more I thought about it, the less sense it made. When had Mom gotten so picky? So touchy? Oh, well.

I resolved to apologize to Mom the moment she got home. And to make it up to her by being extra nice.

My father got home before my mother did.

"Hey, everybody!" he called. By that time, I'd staked out the corner of the sofa in the den and was watching an old movie called *An American in Paris*.

"Hi, Dad," I called.

"Where is everybody?" he said, coming in to sit down next to me.

I kept my eyes on the movie. "Maria is at a post-swim meet practice and Tiffany's in her garden."

The people on the screen began to dance and sing.

My father cleared his throat. "Oh."

"Mom's shopping," I added, still keeping my eyes on the dancing, singing people.

"Oh," said my father again. "Er . . . what meet? What garden?"

That got my attention.

"Maria's swim meet!" I said, staring at him. It was so weird. For a moment, just for a moment, he didn't look like my father. Just a tall man in a cotton sweater and chinos and loafers.

Some stranger. Some stranger who didn't know me or Tiffany or Maria at all.

"Maria's on the swim team at *school*, Dad," I said. "She practices after school practically every day."

"I knew that," said my dad.

But did he?

"And Tiffany started a garden. In the backyard. Haven't you seen it?"

"No. I mean, not exactly."

He sounded just like me when I didn't know the answer to a question when a teacher called on me at school.

We looked at each other for a long moment. Then my father cleared his throat again and bounded up. "Better go get changed," he said and charged out of the room.

Changed into what, I wondered. He's already changed so much. I could understand his not knowing, maybe, about one of Maria's swim meets.

But how could he not have noticed a whole garden in the backyard?

Feeling confused and grumpy, I turned my attention back to the singing, dancing people. Paris, I reminded myself. Think about Paris.

My mother came home from shopping and danced into the den just as the movie came to an end. It was a pretty good movie.

"Hi, Shanny," she sang out. I made a face at the baby name I'd asked her not to call me at least a million times, but I didn't say anything.

"Hi, Mom. Dad's home."

"Great," said my mom. "Look, Shanny."

She put a box down on the coffee table, opened it, and pulled out a dress.

"Is that for you?" I said. "It's nice, Mom." It really was. A sort of Laura Ashley spring dress, with a lace collar and a drop waist and lots of tiny flowers. The kind of dress that looked good on my mom and would look good on Tiffany, too, I thought.

My mom whipped another dress out.

"Here," she said, beaming. "For *you*, Shanny."

I took the dress with a sinking heart, feeling all my resolve fly out the window. My mom had gone shopping and she had bought mother-daughter dresses for me and her, as if I were a little kid. Or a doll.

And she hadn't bought anything like the kind of dress I wore now. But then, I thought hatefully, how would she know? She never listened to me these days, or paid attention to what *I* asked.

"Do you like it?"

What could I say? I didn't like it for me. My mom *must* have known I wouldn't. How could she not? She'd just set herself up — and me, too.

She was looking at me so eagerly that I couldn't say what was on my mind. I felt trapped and angry all over again.

But I said, "It's a very pretty dress, Mom."

Did she notice the lack of enthusiasm in my response? How could she not?

I jumped up. "I'll go hang it in my closet and then after dinner, maybe I can try it on."

I made my escape and that's exactly what it was. An escape. I hung the dress in my closet, resisting the impulse to push it as far to the side as I could. I lay down on my bed and stared at the ceiling.

Not long after, Maria came home. Her hair was dry, but it was slicked back like a seal's.

"Heard you did pretty good," I said, sitting up.

Maria shrugged, but she was smiling.

"So?"

"So, we won," said Maria. She looked up and down the hall, then said, "Can I come in? Your room, I mean."

"Sure," I said.

Maria closed the door behind her and sighed.

"What's up?"

"It's Mom," she said. "I mean, I'm glad she comes to the swim meets and all that, but she . . . she talks to the coach all the time. Coach Williams is a great coach and she's nice to Mom, but none of the other parents do that."

"What does she talk to Coach Williams about?" I asked sympathetically.

"I don't know. But I wish she wouldn't. It's weird. You know?"

"Maybe you could talk to Mom about it," I said.

Maria made a face. "Maybe. But it's like she's not listening, you know?" She sighed heavily and got up. "Oh, well. See you at dinner."

I lay back down and resumed my study of the ceiling of my room. Poor Maria. I knew how she felt. Hedged in. Trapped.

In Paris, I'd be on my own. (Except for the chaperones, of course.) I hated to admit it, but one of the appealing things about Paris these days was just how far I'd be from Mom.

I woke up Sunday morning still brooding over the dress in my closet. It fit. I couldn't even make that excuse for never, ever wearing it.

But I never, ever would.

Maybe I could take it to Paris with me and lose it.

The thought cheered me up. Until the Sunday newspaper incident.

"You should fold the newspaper back when you finish reading it," said Mom. "Other people might want to read it."

"Everyone else has already read it," I said, digging through for the comics.

"You don't know that," said Mom.

"Yes, I do. I asked you. I asked Dad."

"What about Tiffany and Maria?"

"They don't read anything but the comics!"

"Shannon, I think you should put the paper back in order," said Mom.

"Fine," I said through clenched teeth. I put the paper back in order, then marched pointedly through the house and dropped it into the recycling bin. Then I went on marching, out the door. "I'm going over to Kristy's!" I shouted as the door slammed shut behind me.

"Shanny . . ." called my mother.

I didn't answer. I kept going.

"What's wrong?" asked Kristy the moment she opened her door.

"You can tell?"

"Yeah."

"My mom's driving me *crazy*! She treats me like a baby, she doesn't listen to anything I say and she's . . . she's acting like a big baby herself."

"A big baby, huh? Sounds like a job for the BSC," joked Kristy as she led the way to her room.

"Ha," I said sourly. "Do you have the Sunday paper? I didn't even get to read the comics."

"Sure." Kristy detoured through the kitchen, grabbed the comics and a stack of newspaper sections off the top of the pile of newspapers scattered (out of order) on the kitchen table, and kept going.

We went upstairs and scattered sections of newspaper all around the room.

"Nothing about Paris in the travel section," Kristy announced.

"That's okay. I've read a million books about Paris," I told her. "I can hardly wait."

"You are sooo lucky, Shannon. Are you going to get one of those hats?"

"A beret. Yes. Definitely."

Kristy grinned. "Ooh, la, la."

54

We both laughed and scattered some more newspaper sections around in comfortable silence.

And I wondered if the mothers in France ever drove their kids crazy, too.

CHAPTER 5

"The unofficial meeting of the BSC will now come to order," Kristy said, and we all laughed. The time had come to plan the BSC Mother's Day Surprise Extravaganza. So we'd all gone to Kristy's house and, of course, to keep our energy up, we'd just raided the BSC treasury and sent out for pizza.

"A business expense," said Stacey, counting out the money. "Tax deductible."

"We have to keep our strength up," said Claudia. She had come prepared, and since we appreciate the motto, "Life is uncertain, eat dessert first," we were eating out of a bag of Gummi Worms Claud had brought along — except for Stacey, who was eating an apple.

"We always fix our mom breakfast in bed," said Mallory. "For Mother's Day, I mean."

"That's a nice family tradition," said Stacey.

Mallory grinned. "You should see the Pikes getting Mom's breakfast ready!"

The idea of all of the Pike kids in the kitchen at once cooking breakfast for just one person was an awesome one. I had a vision of them passing pancakes down a line, like firefighters in those old movies, passing buckets of water along to put out a fire.

"I bet a lot of kids make Mother's Day breakfasts," said Mary Anne, who was making notes in the club notebook. "We could help kids plan the menus, maybe."

"Mmm. I don't know. It's a good idea, but I don't think it has the 'oomph' we're looking for," Kristy said.

"Oomph?" teased Claudia.

"What about a Saturday Make Your Own Mother's Day Giftathon?" suggested Jessi. "That'd be a lot of fun."

Claudia said (somewhat Gummi Wormily), "Yeah. We could even help them make wrapping paper and cool gift decorations."

"Or the kids could grow a special plant or flower," I suggested, thinking of Tiffany and her garden. Maybe I could get Tiffany involved that way. She'd have other gardeners to talk to (sort of) and get positive reinforcement for her garden.

"So what does our schedule look like, Mary Anne?" asked Kristy briskly. "Can we have this Giftathon soon?"

Mary Anne flipped open the club record

book and ran her finger through the pages, and we settled on a Saturday when we could all get together. We decided on Mary Anne's house, since her backyard is big and we could move to the barn if the weather got bad.

We were idling along on that idea, talking about the supplies we'd need to get and the kinds of presents the kids could make (like a special decorated menu to go with a special Mother's Day breakfast). We discussed whether to let the kids take the gifts home with them then, or arrange to distribute them right before Mother's Day, and congratulated ourselves on how much fun the Giftathon would be, when Kristy got her "Kristy's Great Idea" look on her face.

It was a look we all recognized. Conversation slowed down. Stopped.

Mary Anne said, "Kristy?"

"Hmmmmm," said Kristy slowly, staring at the wall.

We paused expectantly.

Then Kristy said, "Soooo. What about . . . what about a mother-kid softball game? Just for Mother's Day."

"Super!" Claudia was immediately and totally into the idea. She went on, "Now that Stacey and I know all about softball, we could really organize this in a big way."

Claudia was referring to the time she and Stacey took on the job of coaching Kristy's Krushers while Kristy played on the SMS softball team. It had been, well, a learning experience for everyone. And Claudia and Stacey had definitely raised the sense of style for Krushers' softball to a new level.

"Not on Mother's Day," said Jessi. "People should be with their families then. How about sometime after that?"

"Right," said Kristy.

Mary Anne flipped the BSC schedule open again. But the only time that everyone could get together was several weeks later.

"After Mother's Day is fine," Stacey said. "After all, it'll be even warmer and nicer. And we'll need good weather for the game."

"Wait a minute," I said. "I can't make it. I'll be in Paris. Of course, I could cancel my trip, but. . . ."

"Oooh, poor Shannon," teased Stacey. I grabbed a pillow and threw it at Stacey.

Stacey was about to retaliate when the doorbell rang.

"Saved by the bell," I crowed.

"Saved by the pizza," retorted Stacey.

When we'd gotten the pizza and settled down around the big table in Kristy's kitchen, we talked some more about the softball game idea. Claudia suggested we get some white T-shirts and maybe tie-dye them a special color for the mothers' team.

"And the kids can wear their Krushers shirts. We've got a few extras, too, for the kids who aren't on the team," Kristy said.

"What about the kids who are too little to play?" asked Mallory.

"We could make them special cheerleaders," suggested Jessi. "Or offer free babysitting services."

The plans went as fast as the pizza. It sounded like *so* much fun, I really did almost regret I'd have to be in Paris.

Well, okay, I didn't regret that! But I did wish I could be there to see the game.

"I know!" I said. "Maybe someone could videotape the game and then the parents could get copies made. A special Mother's Day memento."

"Super. Absolutely a super idea," cried Kristy, and Mary Anne made another note in the club notebook.

We'd just finished most of the pizza and most of the planning when the doorbell rang.

"More pizza?" cried Claudia happily.

"Claud, you're a bottomless pit," said Stacey.

"Who're you calling a pit?" Claudia made a face as Kristy got up to answer the door.

60

A moment later I froze, my pizza halfway to my mouth.

"Helllooo," called a familiar voice.

My mother's voice. What was *she* doing here?

"Oh, look, pizza!" said my mom brightly, following Kristy into the kitchen.

"Would you like some?" asked Kristy politely.

Silently I willed my mom to say no.

"Well," said my mother, hesitating.

"Come on," said Kristy, pulling up a chair.

I was doomed.

My mom sat down at the table and took a slice of pizza.

I pushed my pizza away. Suddenly, I wasn't hungry anymore.

"Uh, Mom?" I said.

"This is delicious," said my mom.

"It's the black olives and green olives," said Jessi. "That's key."

"And *no* anchovies," said Mallory.

"Uh, Mom?" I tried again.

"Yes?"

"What's going on, Mom?"

"Going on? Oh!" My mom threw back her head and laughed.

I frowned. "Is something wrong? Is that why you're here?" I asked pointedly. And yes, I know, a little rudely.

My mom didn't seem to notice. "No, nothing's wrong. I just need you to come home and watch Tiffany and Maria for an hour or so. I've got to go do some errands and I hate to drag them along with me." My mom made a face. "In fact, I don't think I *could* drag Tiffany away from her garden."

"Why didn't you just call?" I asked, exasperated. The old feeling of being trapped returned.

"Oh, it was no problem." My mom polished off the last of her piece of pizza, stood up, and smiled at everyone. "Thanks for the pizza."

"You're welcome," said Kristy politely.

We sat in silence for a moment. Then I said, not quite looking at Mom, "I'll be home in just a minute, okay?"

At last Mom got that hint. "Okay, Shanny," she said. " 'Bye, guys." She left.

Shanny.

"Shanny?" Kristy gasped.

"Listen, I know my friends are much too sophisticated and kind to go around teasing a person about something like the nickname her mother uses for her," I said.

It didn't work.

"Of course not. Shanny," crooned Stacey.

"Boontsie!" I shot back. That's a name Stacey's father called her when she was a baby.

Stacey clutched her heart. "I'm wounded!"

We all laughed. I looked around the table. We're a great club, if I do say so myself. Even if I was now going to have to hear them use my baby name at probably all the most embarrassing times in my life. Of course, they'd get no mercy back from me.

I stood up reluctantly. "Gotta go," I said. "See you later."

I was almost out the door when they all called out in unison: " 'Bye, *Shannnnnnnnnnnny*."

In spite of the bad mood my mother's visit had put me in, I grinned all the way home.

CHAPTER 6

"Mary had a little lamb, little lamb, little lamb. Mary had a little lamb," I sang under my breath as I hurried down the hall of SDS on the way to the bus after my last class. Only I was trying to sing it in French. But what was the French word for lamb?

"Bah!" I said aloud, and then laughed at my own joke. I'd have to tell that one to Greer.

I raced around the corner, not quite running (running in the halls is frowned on), and skidded to a stop. I reversed and took another look in Dr. Patek's office.

My mother was just inside the door, talking to Dr. Patek.

Huh? Maria's swim meet schedule again? Or had Tiffany had some kind of doctor's appointment I'd forgotten about?

I looked around, but I didn't see Tiff anywhere.

Mary had a little lamb. The words came back

into my head. What *was* the French word for lamb?

Lapin? No, that was rabbit. Mary had a little rabbit?

I was doing that more and more lately. Trying to remember the French words for everything. Even in math, I made myself count as much as possible in French. I wanted to be ready for Paris. It was much nicer to think about Paris than *ma mère* (my mother) so I put her out of my mind as I got on the bus.

Instead I concentrated on practicing my French conversational skills with my friends.

Have you ever tried to gossip in French? When riding a school bus?

"Hey," whispered Meg. She leaned forward. *"Un petit beurre . . ."*

"A little butter?" said Polly.

We went off into gales of laughter. Then we started playing our own version of that road trip game you play when you're a kid: we called our version, "I'm packing for Paris." The way we played was this: Someone started by saying, "I'm packing for Paris and I'm taking an . . ." and she'd name something that began with "a" (in French). The next person had to say the same sentence and word, then add another item. Only this item had to begin with a "b." You just kept going until you got through the alphabet.

Of course, we usually didn't get anywhere near the letter "z," but the game was pretty funny.

This time, we'd made it to a world record — h — when the bus reached my stop.

I was in a great mood. "Hey, I'm home!" I cried as I hit the front door.

Mom had beat me home. She was waiting for me.

"Hey, Mom!" I practically danced into the house. Soon I'd be climbing the Eiffel Tower. Drinking *café au lait* in *un petit bistro*. Wearing a beret bought in Paris.

"Shannon," said my mother and I noticed that she looked as cheerful as I felt. "Guess what?"

"Good news?" I said. I was glad to see Mom looking happy for a change. It probably had something to do with this Friday night. She and Dad had been planning a night out, just the two of them. He'd been trying to get tickets for a play.

I smiled. That was it. He'd gotten the tickets.

I soon found out how wrong I was.

"I'm going to Paris," my mom said.

It took a moment to register. When it did, I felt my mouth drop open — and all my excitement vanish.

But maybe I was jumping to conclusions.

"To Paris?" I repeated, just to make sure.

"Dr. Patek called me down to school this afternoon. She said one of the chaperones for your trip had to cancel and she thought of me as a replacement chaperone. Wasn't that nice of her? So, I'll be going to Paris with you, honey! Isn't that great?"

I once heard someone say, "The world crumbled around her." Well, it's true. It really happens. I could feel my world crumbling around me.

"To Paris," I said, like a broken recording.

"It'll be such fun, Shanny. We'll go sightseeing and shopping. Oh, I can hardly wait."

Paris. My mother was going to Paris. With my friends and me. On *my* trip. The trip I'd been looking forward to practically the whole year.

I felt as if someone was playing some huge, awful joke on me.

You know what I wanted to do, right at that moment, more than anything else in the world? I wanted to throw myself down on the floor and kick my feet and scream and hold my breath until I was blue in the face. I wanted to have a major temper tantrum and scream, like Mallory Pike's little sister, Claire, "No fair! Nofe-air! Nofe-air!"

I took a deep breath.

And the phone rang.

"I got it," shouted Maria. A moment later

she shouted, "Mommmm, it's Daddy!"

Mom reached over and picked up the extension in the kitchen.

"Hi, honey," she said cheerfully.

A moment later she said, "Oh." Her voice didn't sound so cheerful.

Then she said, even more flatly, "Are you sure? Can't they get someone else to . . . oh. Oh. No. No, never mind."

She listened in silence. All the excitement had drained out of her face. "Sure," she said at last. "Another Friday night. Sure."

She hung up the telephone without saying good-bye.

"Friday night is off?" I said cautiously.

My mother nodded, biting her lip. Then she said, "Something's come up. Your father has to go to some deposition."

"I'm sorry," I managed to say.

My mom shrugged. Then she gave me what looked like a forced smile. "Well, we'll always have Paris!"

My smile was just as forced, but I didn't say anything. I couldn't. I couldn't hurt my mother's feelings, especially not right then.

"I'd better go study," I said.

I studied. I studied French. I studied math. I studied astronomy. I read a short story for English.

I got my French translation right. I solved

every single math problem. I answered the study questions for astronomy. I wrote a paragraph about my favorite character in the short story.

My homework was perfect. I knew all the answers.

So why didn't I know the answer to this one: what was I going to do about my mother going to Paris with me?

No answer for that. No answer because there was nothing I could do.

Grow up, Shannon, I told myself. You are sooo lucky. Most kids, most *people*, never have the chance to go to Paris at all.

It'll be great. Your friends will be there. You'll have a blast.

But was I listening to myself? I was not. Because I knew it wasn't going to do any good.

My trip to Paris had been ruined.

CHAPTER 7

Saturday

The Mother's Day surprize Giftathone was great. Terific. And I liked being the boss. Exxcept when the eggs got brokken. And all the refreshmints. Turst Jacky!...

They started arriving at Mary Anne's at one o'clock sharp: dozens and dozens of kids (or at least it seemed that way), all ready and eager to make the perfect Mother's Day gift.

Fortunately, the day was a nice one. The BSC had set up card tables and picnic tables outside in Mary Anne's huge yard. Different tables were for different kinds of projects: making jewelry and special cards and decorating boxes and cans and blowing out eggs to make special Mother's Day ornaments to hang up all year-round. And one of the picnic tables had been converted into a potting table, with Tiffany in charge. We'd collected a gazillion coffee cans so the kids could decorate them and use them as flowerpots.

At first it hadn't been easy to convince Tiffany to join in the BSC extravaganza. But when I took her with Kristy and me to the gardening center and started asking for help in choosing the right kinds of seeds for Mother's Day plants, she was hooked.

Stacey met people as they arrived and got their contribution (we charged everyone a dollar to help pay for all the supplies).

"Good crowd," I said to Kristy. We were at the box-and-can decorating table.

"I am going to make an eyeglass case for my mother," announced Karen.

Kristy looked doubtfully at the stack of boxes. "I don't know, Karen. These boxes are pretty big for an eyeglass case."

"I'm going to fold some cardboard," Karen explained. "And glue it so it is shaped like my eyeglass case, see?" She dug in her backpack and produced a bright blue eyeglass case.

"And it's going to be gigundoly beautiful," said Karen. "With sequins *and* feathers." She paused and studied her own eyeglass case for a minute, then put it on the table in front of her. "And maybe I'll decorate mine, too."

One table away, standing by Mallory, Claudia was trying to keep an eye on all the tables at once while helping two of the Pike triplets make a special Mother's Day breakfast menu-and-card combination.

"I think it should look like a real menu," Byron was arguing. "Like those menus in fancy restaurants. You know, the kind with the tassels in them."

"She's not going to order from it," argued his brother Jordan. "It's just a special card, so she'll remember what she had for breakfast. Making a whole big menu for orange juice and waffles and syrup . . ."

"Three kinds of syrup!"

"Okay, three kinds of syrup, but that's going to look weird."

Claudia said, "If we write it in really elegant script, I bet it'll look fine."

"Will you write it?"

Claudia thought for a minute, then nodded. "But only if someone else spells it!" she warned.

Tiffany was showing Hannie and Linny Papadakis how to plant zinnia seeds in a pot. "They're very hardy," she was explaining. "And they make a nice cut flower."

"I want pink ones," said Hannie.

"Here are some pink ones. Little pink ones. The seeds inside this package will grow up to be just like the picture on the package," said Tiffany. "And look at the seeds. They come from right in the middle of the flower, so when the flowers bloom, look for them. You can even save the seeds from one year to the next."

I smiled to myself. That was the most talking I had heard Tiffany do in a long time.

Claudia left her table to check on the others and make sure that everyone had supplies and knew what they were doing. It was while she was at the jewelry table with Mary Anne, showing Maria how to make feather earrings, that the egg incident occurred.

It started as an accident. A Jackie Rodowsky-the-walking-disaster accident.

We all love Jackie, don't get me wrong. But Jackie has a special knack for causing, well, unexpected things to happen. For instance, he'll walk across a room and somehow a table will tip over and a zillion magazines will go slithering to the floor.

Or he'll hit a baseball and knock a branch off a tree and the branch will fall and break the rearview mirror off a parked car.

He never means for things to happen. They just do.

This time, Jackie (who was at the egg decorating table with Mary Anne and Jessi) and Adam Pike somehow got a couple of the eggs away from one of the cartons. The next thing we knew, they were having an egg race, trying to walk across the yard with an egg balanced on two fingers of one hand.

"Jackie, no!" cried Claudia.

But it was too late. Looking down at the egg on his fingers (miraculously still there), Jackie never saw the table with the refreshments that Stacey and Jessi had just started setting up.

He walked right into the table.

Jessi was headed back into the house for the cookies, but Stacey, who was behind the table, had just bent over to pick up a plastic jug of lemonade. She straightened up and saw the whole table, with Jackie on top, come hurtling toward her. She made a mad grab for the table, forgetting that she'd loosened the top on the lemonade.

Sticky pink lemonade splashed out over everyone.

Eggs flew in the air. They crashed down on top of Stacey and Adam and Jackie.

All the kids began to shriek excitedly. For a minute or two, pandemonium reigned.

Then Kristy shouted, "QUIET!"

And it worked. She grinned. "Over to you, Claudia," she said.

"Oh, wow," said Claudia. She looked all around, then said, "Okay, everybody, go on and keep working on your presents — unless you want to help me clean up this mess."

Everybody instantly became *very* interested in the projects on which they'd been working.

Claudia began helping Stacey, Jackie, and Adam to their feet.

"Cool," said Adam. He was covered with pink lemonade and he had egg on one shoulder of his T-shirt.

Jackie looked worried, but not upset. Being involved in disasters was nothing new for him. "Gosh," was all he said.

What could anyone say?

Stacey rubbed her hand through her hair and said, "I hear a lemon rinse brings out the shine in your hair. I don't know about lemonade, though."

Mary Anne came over. "Dawn left some clothes here that would probably fit you," she told Stacey. "Jeans and shirts. And I know Jeff left some old T-shirts you guys can put on."

"I'll take care of the refreshments," said Jessi, trying hard not to laugh. "Don't worry."

A little while later, Adam and Jackie came out fairly well cleaned and scrubbed, followed by Stacey (in an old T-shirt of Dawn's that said "Surf's Up"), and Mary Anne.

By then, people were trying on earrings and necklaces they'd made, proudly displaying flowerpots filled with potting soil, and beginning to wrap the gifts they'd made for their mothers.

It was quite a collection, too. Karen's idea to make an eyeglass case had inspired half a dozen copies, all lavishly painted and sprinkled with sequins and glitter. One of the coffee can flowerpots had the instructions for taking care of the seed planted inside, decoupaged to the outside. Byron and Jordan Pike's menu boasted elegant gold script and they folded it in half just like in a restaurant. On the outside were the words: *Special Order for a Special Mom.*

"Look, Shannon." Maria held up a pair of earrings made with feathers. "Do you think Mom will like them?"

"She'll love them," I said, and I knew she would.

"I'm going to wrap them, then," said Maria, and hurried away.

The action at the plant table seemed to have slowed down. I watched as Tiffany carefully scraped the extra potting soil back into the bags and neatly folded down the tops of the partially used seed bags.

"How'd it go?" I asked.

Tiffany looked up and nodded, trying to look serious. Then her face lit up with a huge grin. "It was fun," she said simply.

Looking around at the swirl of activity and listening to the hum of contented laughter and talk, I had to agree with her. It was fun. And a lot of mothers were going to get wonderful, funny, lopsided, love-filled gifts for Mother's Day. And I was sure they were going to love them.

Claudia stepped to the middle of the yard and clapped her hands. "Attention, everybody, attention!"

Gradually, everyone turned to look at her.

"You did great!" Claudia said. "Label each of your gifts with your name and put them on the picnic table over there under the big tree. We'll see that you get them back the day before Mother's Day.

"And let's see, what else. Hmmm. I know it was important . . ."

Claudia looked at the sky. She looked down at her feet. Then she slapped her forehead. "Oh, yeah! I almost forgot! Refreshments are now being served!"

CHAPTER 8

Mother's Day.

M-Day.

A bad day.

It didn't start out that way. In fact, it had gotten off to a pretty good start the day before. We'd gathered all the gifts the kids had made and labeled and stored them in Mary Anne's old barn. All of the plants had started coming up and some even had their first blooms on them. (Tiffany had been instrumental in reminding us to keep the plants watered and put them where they'd get enough light.) The kids had all been delighted and excited and could hardly wait until the next day.

Mary Anne had laughingly confessed that she'd made Mother's Day gifts this year for her stepmother and her father: a basket for her stepmother (who is a little absentminded) to put all her mail in, and cedar sachets for her father's dresser drawers.

Everyone else had bought their gifts, including me: perfume, my mother's favorite kind, in a special Mother's Day box and shiny department store wrapping.

But I had made a card on my own.

Things had been even more tense than usual around our house. I'd been avoiding Mom, and avoiding talking about Paris. I'd been trying not to think of it at all.

But I knew that Dad and Mom hadn't made up after the date that Dad had to break with Mom. I felt bad for Mom. It seemed like nothing was going right for her.

On M-Day, Sunday, I got up extra early and woke up Maria and Tiffany. Together we went quietly downstairs to the kitchen and set up our presents on the table: the perfume with my card; Maria's gift, a neatly wrapped box in handmade wrapping paper containing the feather earrings she'd made (plus a special card decorated with feathery designed cutouts); and a vase that Tiffany had bought, filled with fresh flowers picked from her own garden.

"It looks beautiful," I said, stepping back to admire our handiwork.

"Shhh!" said Maria. "I hear someone!"

Sure enough, Mom came into the kitchen a moment later, yawning. She walked over to the counter, filled the coffeemaker pot with water, then stopped.

Slowly she turned around, still yawning, and stared at us and the table.

"What is this?" she said, but she was beginning to smile through her yawns.

"Happy Mother's Day!" we cried.

"What beautiful flowers. And that vase . . ."

"From me," said Tiffany, beaming. "The flowers are from my garden."

"Are they really? I had no idea you had such a wonderful garden, honey. These are incredible!" My mom reached out and touched the velvety petal of a jonquil in wonder.

"Here, Mom," said Maria, not to be outdone. She thrust the package and card into Mom's hands. "I made it myself. Even the wrapping paper!"

"The paper too? Then I'll be very careful." Slowly, delicately, Mom unwrapped Maria's present. I thought Maria would burst with excitement before Mom got it undone. She held the feather earrings up and they danced in the light.

"They're dyed feathers," said Maria. "Especially for making jewelry. I knew green was your favorite color, so I mixed all the greens together."

"Beautiful," murmured Mom, fastening the

earrings to her ears. "And what's this?"

"From me," I told her.

She unwrapped the perfume and exclaimed, "My favorite kind. I was almost out. I was trying to wait until I got to Paris, but now I don't have to! Thank you!"

Forcing myself not to think about Paris, I leaned over and kissed Mom on the cheek. "You're welcome."

"I'll go get Dad," said Maria.

It was just at that moment, while Mom was admiring the cards, that I saw the note stuck to the refrigerator with a magnet. I recognized my father's handwriting with a sinking heart.

"Wait a minute," I said.

"What is it?" asked Mom. She saw the direction in which I was looking and watched in silence as I took the note off the refrigerator door.

"It's from Dad," I said, reading it. I handed it to Mom. "He's playing golf."

"He forgot?" said Maria indignantly. "He forgot Mother's Day?"

Mom looked crestfallen. Quickly I said, "I know! Let's all go out to lunch when Dad gets home. That'll be fun."

"Yeah!" said Maria.

Tiffany nodded, looking happier.

And most importantly, Mom looked a little

less glum. "Okay!" she said. "Yes. Let's do that. We'll make your father treat us all to an extra-special meal for forgetting."

We laughed then, but I stopped laughing when Mom turned to me and said, "And we can wear our new dresses, Shannon."

Oh, no! I was hoping she had forgotten those dresses. I said quickly, "It's, uh, it's at the cleaners, Mom."

"Oh. Well, I'll wear mine, anyway," said Mom.

Whew, that had been a close call. I was glad Mom didn't seem to really mind.

Unfortunately, since my dress was not (of course) at the cleaners I got caught in the lie when Mom went upstairs right before lunch to put some clean clothes in my closet. I'd hung up the dress and I'd pushed it to one side of my closet, but not far enough.

"Shannon?" said my mom's muffled voice as I walked down the hall.

"What is it, Mom?" I asked.

"I'm in here. In your room. And so is . . . this." Mom backed out of the closet and held up the dress.

I looked at it. I looked at her.

What could I say? "I *thought* it was at the cleaners," I said.

Mom didn't answer. She just turned and put the dress back in the closet. "Your socks are on the bed," she said, and walked away.

I could hardly wait for Dad to get home. Anything was bound to be an improvement.

And this time, I was almost right.

Dad showed up holding a big, gorgeously wrapped box. "I'm sorry, sweetheart," he told Mom. "It was just such a perfect day for golf. But I didn't forget Mother's Day."

My mother's face was all smiles. "You didn't," she said. "And you're going to take us out to lunch to celebrate, too."

"It's a deal," said my dad. "Go on, open it."

Smiling, Mom pulled the card out from under the paper and opened it.

It was as if someone had reached over and wiped the smile off her face. She looked up at my father and said, "Happy birthday?"

My father's face turned bright red.

Mom threw the card in the air. "What is this? An emergency gift you keep in your office in case you forget some occasion or someone gives you a gift and you don't have one for them?"

Dad's face turned even redder and I knew it was true. My mom went on, "You could at least have gotten the card right! Thanks a *lot*."

Mom jumped up and ran out of the kitchen. Dad hurried after her. "Sweetheart, wait a minute. Let me explain," my sisters and I heard him say.

"Don't sweetheart me! You don't have to explain *anything*!"

"I don't know about you guys," I said, "but I'm going to go to my room."

"I wish I could go to swim practice," said Maria gloomily, following me, on the way to her room. Behind us, we heard the back door click shut and knew that Tiffany had headed out to her garden.

We ended up going out to lunch after all. Mom and I even wore our mother-daughter dresses. And Mom wore her earrings, pinned one of the flowers from Tiffany's bouquet to her dress, and made everyone smell her wrist which she'd dabbed with perfume.

Dad made a lot of jokes and laughed at everything we said.

It wasn't much fun. I was glad when lunch was over. I couldn't decide which was worse: the long silences, or the way everybody was trying so hard to act as if everything was all right, talking and laughing and being nervous and strange.

And I hated the way I looked in my new dress.

It was a huge relief to finally get home and

take the dress off and retreat to my room again.

Until Mom knocked on the door.

"Thanks for the perfume, Shannon," she said.

"You're welcome, Mom," I replied (for about the thousandth time). "I'm glad you like it."

"You looked lovely in your dress," she went on.

"It's a pretty dress," I said as neutrally as possible. So I thought it was much nicer on the hanger than on me. So what?

"Are you studying?" asked Mom.

I shrugged. "Just reading."

"Shouldn't you be studying for exams?"

I'd already made my final exam study plans and was about to tell Mom that, but she rushed on, "You need to set up a schedule. You should allow a certain amount of time for each subject. Also, do you have your old tests from your courses? Tests are a very important study tool . . ."

"Mom! Stop it! *Stop it!*"

"But, Shannon!"

Goaded, I snapped, "I've got a study schedule set up, okay, Mom? I *know* how to study! Or haven't you noticed that I make good grades?"

"I was only trying to help."

I didn't answer. I couldn't think of anything to say. At least, not that I could say aloud.

After a long moment of silence, Mom left.

I closed my eyes and groaned. It had been a rotten, disgusting, horrible day.

And it didn't help that I'd been so awful to my mom, who'd had an even worse day than I had.

A Mother's Day to forget.

CHAPTER 9

I couldn't believe school was almost over. I thought time was supposed to fly when you were having fun, *not* when you were studying every spare second for finals.

Which is what I'd been doing, right on schedule. And I hadn't forgotten to schedule some free time, so I wouldn't be completely burnt out.

Of course, Mom found me once when I was lying on my stomach on the rug reading a magazine. She didn't believe I was taking a legitimate study break. She thought I was goofing off. That really annoyed me. Why would I lie about something like that? I cared as much about school and making good grades as my mom did.

We didn't speak for a whole day after that.

I almost enjoyed it.

Polly and Lindsey and Greer and Meg were all *totally* into the Paris trip. It was all they talked about. And the more they talked about it, the more I couldn't.

I'd mentioned that my mom was going to chaperone. "Bummer," said Greer. "But at least your mom's not some weirdo or something."

"But she's my *mom*," I'd cried.

Lindsey had patted my shoulder sympathetically. "Hey, Paris is a big city," she said. "You probably won't even know she's there."

"And we'll protect you," Polly joked.

I smiled wanly. They didn't understand how trapped and angry I felt and I didn't know if I wanted them to. I didn't talk about it again.

But I never, ever thought I would hate and despise the idea of going to Paris. That I would wake up in the middle of the night thinking, *"Non, non, non!"*

I'd dreamed about Paris all year. And now it was turning into a nightmare. I didn't know what to do.

Until I had my great idea.

"Bonjour, mademoiselle," said Madame as she put the French final facedown on the desk in front of me. She gave us our instructions and we turned the tests over.

Quickly I ran my eyes down the test. And knew that I could ace it *facilement*.

I picked up my pencil and began writing.

Only most of the answers I wrote down were wrong.

I walked out of my class in a daze. I'd just done something I'd never done before in my life.

I'd flunked a test. And I'd done it on purpose.

I didn't tell anybody I'd flunked. Everyone would know soon enough, when the grades were posted.

Five days later, as I joined the crowd around the bulletin board in the front hall at school, I heard my name being called over the PA system to report to the office.

Quickly I found what I was looking for: my final grades were three A's, two B's, and an F. The F was in French.

When I got to the office, I wasn't surprised to see Dr. Patek, Madame DuBarry, and Ms. Danvers, the guidance counselor, all waiting in the principal's office.

"Come in, Shannon, and close the door," said Dr. Patek, looking serious. "Have a seat."

Dr. Patek made a tent with her fingers. "Have you seen the final grades posted in the front hall, Shannon?"

I nodded.

"What happened?" asked Madame DuBarry. "You are such a good student —

and then to flunk your final so badly!"

"Are there problems you'd like to discuss?" suggested Ms. Danvers. She had a kind face, but how could I tell her that my mother was the reason I'd flunked my exam — not for any horrible reason, but just so I wouldn't have to travel with her to Paris, just so I could have some space?

"I guess I didn't study hard enough," I said at last. It didn't sound convincing, but it was the best I could do.

Dr. Patek sighed. "Very well," she said. "Shannon, you know that going to Paris requires keeping your grades up. You haven't met that criteria. I am sorry to have to tell you this, but you are not eligible for the trip. You can't go."

It felt bad, but it felt good, too. I tried not to look triumphant.

But I'd done it. I'd gotten out of the trip. I could spend the time with my friends, hang out, enjoy myself. Without my mother hovering nearby, telling me what to do.

None of my friends at SDS could understand it, of course. I didn't try to explain. I just kept saying over and over, "I froze. All the French went out of my head. I guess I didn't study enough."

"We'll send you a zillion postcards," Polly promised.

"And bring you French chocolates," said Greer.

"You better!" I said.

Mom was waiting for me when I got home. I could tell by her face that she'd already heard the news. I told her what I'd told everyone else.

Studying me intently, Mom shook her head. "I don't know what to think, Shannon. I find it very hard to believe that you could flunk one subject like that, a subject at which you worked extra hard. But maybe you don't want to go to Paris, hard as I find that to believe. I also find it hard to believe that you wouldn't say something."

That made me feel guilty, but I didn't answer.

Mom shook her head again, then went on. "Well, I've promised I'd chaperone. And I still want to go to Paris. So I'm going. Meanwhile, since you are going to be at home, and since you are an experienced baby-sitter, I've leaving you in charge of Tiffany and Maria and the house during the day. Your father will be home at night, and the housekeeper will be here. We'll arrange for her to come over every day and she'll leave meals for all of you when she's here. But you'll be responsible for the grocery lists, the shopping, and making sure that everything goes smoothly."

I was stunned. *This* from my mother, who kept telling me how to do every little thing? Who treated me like a baby? Who spent her whole life, it seemed, interfering in mine?

"Well, Shannon?" said my mother.

I found my voice at last. "Fine," I said.

Au revoir, Paris.

CHAPTER 10

The first day of a school year is always exciting. And the last day is always sad, at least for me. Not that I don't look forward to summer, because I do.

But I like school, too.

The last day of school is pretty cool, too, at SDS. We don't have to wear our uniforms, for one thing. So we wear our scruffiest jeans and brightest, loudest colors and lace bells into our sneakers and all kinds of silly stuff. The teachers get into the spirit, too. Our principal always shows up in a really outrageous hat. This year, our math teacher had on a T-shirt that said, "2 + 2 = *what*????" Our PE teacher organized a short volleyball game — with balloons — before we cleaned out our lockers.

Greer and I could hear the balloons popping as we sat in front of our gym lockers.

"I *think* this was a gym sock," Greer reported, holding out a wadded-up brownish-yellowish clump of terrycloth.

"I don't think it can be saved," I answered. I finished stuffing my gear into the plastic bag I'd brought along for the occasion, and put it in the bottom of my backpack.

We wandered back upstairs toward the lunchroom.

It was pizza day, just like always on the last day of school. I spotted Dr. Patek's hat (shaped like a pickle this year) ahead of us on line. Greer and I grabbed slices of pizza and milk (no soda, even on the last day of school!) and we settled down with Lindsey and Polly.

"Lundi en Paris, oui?" said Polly.

"No French, no Paris talk," I warned, only half kiddingly. "And yes, I know you'll be in Paris on Monday."

Some of the teachers got serious and gave us talks about how much it meant to teach us. Our philosophy teacher did; so did our math teacher, who got kind of choked up. It was corny, but it kind of choked me up, too. It's funny. You don't expect math teachers to be sentimental.

It seemed like only yesterday that I started the school year, only yesterday that I couldn't believe a summer had gone by so fast and that I was starting school again already, only yesterday that Mom was lining us up in our school uniforms for our annual first-day-of-school photograph.

I'd never see some of these teachers again, maybe. One year, I had come back to school to find one of my favorite teachers, my English teacher, had married and moved to Minnesota, where his wife had found a job.

We got out of our last class early so we could clean out our lockers. As an organized person, I'd already done a lot of the cleaning out. As a person who wasn't quite ready for the end of the school year, I still had a ways to go: notebooks with a couple of blank pages in them, notes that I'd never finished, magazines, half packs of gum (not that we're allowed to chew gum at SDS).

I tore down a magazine photo of the Paris skyline and wadded it up. I'd had it up in the back of my locker since the Paris trip had first been mentioned.

At last I was through.

We walked outside and got on the bus home. Greer and Polly and Lindsey and Meg talked top speed about Monday and Paris. For them, summer was beginning and ending with that trip. I understood that. But I wasn't a part of it.

I leaned back and stared out the window. I was sorry school was over. But it was time.

"See you guys *après* Paris," I said as I left the bus.

"*Au revoir! À bientôt*, Shannon!" they screamed out the widow as the bus pulled away.

I waved. Beside me, Maria and Tiffany stopped to wave, too.

No homework. No books. Lots of unstructured, guiltless free time ahead, beginning now.

"So what're you going to do?" I asked my sisters when we got home.

Tiffany said, "My garden needs weeding," and whisked around the side of the house. I realized in amusement that the clothes she'd chosen for grunge wear on the last day of school were true grunge wear — her gardening clothes.

Maria said, "I don't know. I've never liked any sport but swimming. But it's important that you stay in shape. I was thinking of cross-training this summer."

"Cross-training?" For some reason, the idea of Maria voluntarily doing any other sport but swimming did not compute. "Like what?"

"I don't know. Skating. Rollerblading, maybe. Bicycling. I have to think about it first. And talk to Coach."

"Good luck," I said.

"Yeah," said Maria.

I looked at my watch. Not even near five-thirty yet. Not even near time for the Friday meeting of the BSC. I sighed. School was over. I could *feel* my mother hovering somewhere in the house, not intentionally trying to get on my nerves any more than I was trying to get on hers. But it would happen just the same, and most of my SDS friends were headed out for Paris in just three days, along with my mother.

I wasn't going to get a vacation in Paris, but I definitely needed a vacation — from my life. And it looked like hanging out with my BSC friends was the closest I was going to get.

"This meeting of the BSC will now come to order."

Music to my ears. I took a handful of Cheez Doodles out of the bag Claudia was passing around and settled back blissfully.

"Any new business?" Kristy went on.

Stacey said, "I'm pleased to report that the Make-a-Giftathon was a success. And we have some arts and crafts supplies left over."

"Like eggs?" suggested Mallory slyly. We all hooted.

"The response to the mother-kid softball team has been super," said Mary Anne, consulting the record book. "So far we've got

Buddy and Suzi Barrett and their mother; David Michael and your mother, Kristy; Hannie and Linny Papadakis and their mother; the Pikes; Haley and Matt Braddock and their mother; Jackie, Shea, and Archie Rodowsky and their mother; Charlotte Johanssen and her mother; and Marilyn and Carolyn Arnold and their mother."

"And my sister Maria — and me," I said.

Mary Anne looked confused. "You're playing?" she asked.

"Well, Maria wants to play and Mom's going to be away, so I thought I'd take her place in the game," I suggested.

"I don't see any problem with that," said Kristy.

The others nodded.

"Great," I said.

Kristy continued. "This is a terrific response, but it's going to take some *serious* organizing." She didn't sound worried. After all, she could look around the room and find seven experienced baby-sitters to help out!

We settled in, between taking calls and booking sitting jobs, to figure out the details, such as who would be in charge of refreshments (Claudia volunteered for that, naturally), who was going to be on what team (the BSC members would have to play on the parents' team, since clearly the kids were going to outnumber their moms), and who was going to umpire.

"Bart said he'd be glad to ump," said Kristy. "I kind of mentioned it to him the other day. I thought he'd be more impartial than any of us."

She paused, as if daring us to give her grief about Bart, who is her sort of boyfriend (as well as the coach of the Krushers' rival softball team, the Bashers), but none of us did. I guess we were still in our mellow last-day-of-school mode.

"We need at least one more umpire, don't you think?" said Stacey.

"True," said Kristy. "But who?"

"Logan and his family are going to be away that weekend," said Mary Anne regretfully.

"I know! I'll ask Nannie," said Kristy. "She'll make a great umpire."

"Perfect," said Mary Anne, making more notes in the record book.

We decided on lemonade, popcorn, boxes of raisins, orange slices, and ginger ale, and diet soda at the refreshment stand. Claudia and Mallory decided to take turns running it and keeping the cashbox. Claudia had gotten some T-shirt paint and was going to design a logo that said "BSC Mother's Day Game" and stencil it on the backs of T-shirts for the mothers' team to wear. Each family that entered was required to donate a large, plain white crew neck T-shirt. That was the entry fee.

The kids were going to wear Krushers' shirts.

And we decided to use Krusher rules. Krusher rules are pretty loose. For instance, we use a Wiffle ball for the littlest kids. And they get more strikes. Things like that.

"Take me out to the ball game," sang Jessi.

"Play ball," answered Kristy.

CHAPTER 11

For once, we were all sitting at the breakfast table together. It was the morning that my mother was leaving town to go on *my* vacation to Paris.

It was your choice, I told myself, staring down into my glass of orange juice. Paris will still be there. And you'll be there someday soon.

"Did I write down your flight number?" my mother was saying to my father.

"Yes, and I wrote yours down, too. In two different places."

Not only was my mother going to Paris, but my father was going away on business the week after that. He and Mom would see each other in the airport as Dad was leaving and Mom was returning, so Dad was going to give Mom his parking ticket when he met her and she was going to drive the car home from the airport. That meeting in the airport was the only time they were going to see each other for two whole weeks.

I wondered if that was the longest they'd been apart since they'd been married.

"The bus is picking us all up at Stoneybrook Day School and taking us to the airport," my mother said for about the thousandth time, (and pulling the ticket out of her purse and checking it for the thousandth time, too).

"Relax," my dad told her. "They won't leave without you. You're a chaperone! You have one of the most important jobs on the trip."

My mother smiled. "It is a job, isn't it? But it doesn't feel like one. I'm so excited."

My dad smiled back. "Well, part of your job on this trip, anyway, is to have a great time." He reached out and patted my mom's hand and they smiled at each other.

After breakfast, we helped load Mom's luggage into the car.

"Aren't you coming, Shannon?" asked my mother as I closed the car door and stepped back.

I shook my head. I'd planned on going to see my mom off at school, and my friends, too. But now, at the last minute, I just couldn't do it. I'd managed to stay pretty neutral about not going to Paris, but I didn't know how I'd feel standing there waving as they all drove away and left me.

"Well, don't forget to get fresh milk, one percent for your father, whole milk for you kids. And Astrid's due for her weekly bath. Her shampoo is in the bathroom cabinet on the left. No, no, it's on the right. You'll see it. And don't use the good towels. I use the dark towels at the bottom of the linen closet for Astrid. Oh, yes, the latch on the dishwasher needs adjusting. The repair service is supposed to call to set up an appointment, but the dishwasher works if you jiggle the latch. And make sure Maria and Tiffany take their vitamins, and you, too . . . and your father knows . . ."

"Mom, it's only a week," I said. "Dad'll be home every night. I have his office number, and he's got a beeper, okay? And Mrs. Bryar will be coming in extra days for the housekeeping and cooking, so we'll be fine. Okay?"

"But, Shanny!"

"See you in a little while, kiddo," said my dad, winking and putting the car in reverse.

"Have fun!" I called as the car backed out of the drive.

"Be careful!" my mom called back.

Be careful? What did that mean?

For a moment I contemplated the possibility that my mom had rigged booby traps in the house. I imagined opening the linen closet door and being conked on the head by a falling ironing board.

But that was impossible. I knew perfectly well that the ironing board stayed in the laundry room, all set up and ready for ironing.

What did my mother think was going to happen?

Be careful. Hmmm.

I knew, I thought, why my parents had put me in charge rather than keeping the sitter they had hired. They were teaching me a lesson: about maturity, about responsibility, about how difficult running a house is, and, by extension how difficult being a parent and being in charge are.

They were teaching me a lesson. And they expected me to fail.

Well, I might have failed French. But that was on purpose. I wasn't about to fail at this.

I walked back in the house and looked around. Everything neat and tidy. The dishes in the sink caught my eye and I whisked them into the dishwasher. Mrs. Bryar was coming in the afternoon to do some laundry and straightening up, and to cook dinner. She was coming three full days this week and two half days.

I went upstairs and got my notebook and my calendar and sat down to polish my housekeeping list.

My housekeeping notebook. Mary Anne's devotion to the BSC record book and the BSC's perfect record in keeping sitting jobs organized had not escaped me. In my housekeeping notebook, I'd written down all the emergency numbers — doctor, vet, fire department, police department, poison control center, and plumber. I'd written in the days Mrs. Bryar was coming to do housekeeping. I'd written in her phone number. I wrote in now, on Thursday, *Bathe Astrid*. I wrote at the top of each day, *Vitamins.* On Tuesday and Friday, I wrote, *Water Plants.*

I was going to go over my list with Mrs. Bryar and try to plan menus for the week. Mrs. Bryar was cooking dinners during the week, but there was still the weekend. And lunch. And breakfast.

But I was prepared. And organized. Nothing was going to go wrong.

I was home alone when I heard the rustling in the bushes. The dishwasher was loaded, the house was clean, and I was on the couch in the den reading a murder mystery and waiting for Mrs. Bryar to show up.

Rustle, rustle.

Why hadn't Astrid barked? She was supposed to be a good watch dog!

Then I remembered that Maria had taken

Astrid with her to the park. She was going to try to teach Astrid to pull her on roller skates. Cross-training apparently could involve dogs.

Cautiously I got up. The sound was coming from underneath the window. I pulled the curtain back and tried to see into the bushes below.

I saw a faint movement, a hand. . . . Someone was hiding in the bushes by the house!

Dial 911! I thought. But I couldn't move.

Suddenly whoever was crouching in the bushes straightened up and I found myself face-to-face with —

The meter reader from the power company.

I stifled a shriek just in time. The meter reader looked sort of startled herself. Then she smiled. "Hi," she called through the glass.

"Uh, hi,"I said weakly. Boy was I glad I hadn't screamed.

"Everything seems to be in order," she said.

"Great," I managed to say.

She waved and stepped out of the bushes and disappeared around the house.

I fell back onto the sofa. I had just gotten relaxed when the sound of Mrs. Bryar's key in the lock caused me to jump a mile.

"Mrs. Bryar?"

"Who else would it be?" said Mrs. Bryar, a laugh in her voice.

"Right," I said. I got up and went to meet her and see about planning menus for the week (and a grocery list).

On my calendar, under Monday, I wrote, *Meter Reader*.

Grocery shopping Tuesday morning took a little longer than I expected. For one thing, I had Maria and Tiffany with me. I was surprised, when I suggested they come with me, that they both agreed readily. Enthusiastically, even. I thought perhaps the idea of riding the town bus to and from the grocery store appealed to them.

I quickly found out otherwise.

"Oooh," said Maria as we entered the supermarket. "Can we just buy frozen dinners, Shannon? I love frozen dinners. Especially the steak ones."

"Oh, no. Mom expects us to eat normal food. You know she doesn't feed us frozen dinners, and I'm not going to either."

"Just one," wheedled Maria.

"Just none," I answered.

Pouting, Maria trailed after me down the aisles.

Tiffany wanted to buy a different kind of breakfast cereal — the kind where sugar is the first and second ingredient listed on the label.

"No," I said. "I don't want Mom coming home and asking me what we're doing with a box of Sugar Krunchies on the shelf."

"We'll throw away what we don't eat before she gets back."

"No, Tiffany."

Tiffany didn't pout. She just moved on to the next goal.

Maria stopped pouting when we reached the bread section, with the economy sized jelly rolls. She spent fifteen minutes trying to convince me that as an athlete, she needed jelly rolls more than any other food on earth.

By the time we left the grocery store I had said no not only to frozen dinners and Sugar Krunchies, but to the giant economy sized can of candied popcorn, live lobsters, three kinds of cookies, and every bag of candy on a discount candy table.

And I'd forgotten the furniture polish that Mrs. Bryar had specifically requested. I'd arranged to have the groceries delivered, but when I called and asked them to add the furniture polish to the list, someone with a bored voice told me the morning deliveries had gone out.

Before I turned around in disgust to make a mad dash back to the store, I wrote, *Groc Shop* on my calendar in the Tuesday morning section.

It was a good thing I did go back and get the polish. Because the grocery delivery person hadn't arrived by the time Mrs. Bryar left.

He didn't arrive until half an hour later. I threw open the door. "It's about time," I said. "We could've starved! It's a good thing there was enough meat in the freezer for meatloaf!"

The guy gave me a funny look. "Uh, could you sign here, please?"

Impatiently, I signed my name. "Just put it on the counter in the kitchen."

"The counter?"

What was wrong with him? "Yes, please." I turned and walked toward the kitchen. A few moments later, I heard him following me.

"Over here." I gestured toward the kitchen counter and stepped aside.

The delivery man staggered in under the weight of his delivery — and dropped fifty pounds of Astrid's dog food on the kitchen counter.

"Have a nice day," he said, and walked out.

I stood and stared at the bag for a long time. Where were our groceries? Did Mom have a regular order of dog food delivered? How could she have forgotten to tell me that?

The kitchen door opened and Astrid came sailing in, pulling Maria on her roller skates. "I'm home," Maria said.

"Take your skates off in the house," I said.

"Tiff? Tiffannny!" called Maria, skating around and around the table.

"Maria, I mean it," I said, watching in dismay as little lines began to appear on Mrs. Bryar's newly mopped floor.

"Okay, okay." Maria went back outside and I heard her talking to Astrid as she pulled her skates off. Then I heard her say, "Hey, Tiff, there you are!"

That took care of them, at least for the time being. She ran to join Tiffany in her garden.

I grabbed some towels and tried to get up the marks from the roller skates. That worked pretty well. (I wrote in my calendar: *Groc: Paper Towels*.)

But when I tried to lift the dog food off the counter, I couldn't hold it. It fell to the floor and broke open. Dog food went everywhere.

I was still chasing dog food nuggets around the kitchen when Maria and Tiffany came in. Astrid came with them. She was wearing baby clothes!

"Don't do that to Astrid," I said. "It makes her look undignified."

Just then Astrid gave an undignifed woof and a jump and knocked the bag of dog food (now sitting on the floor) over again.

I barely cleaned it up before Dad came home.

My experience wasn't Paris, but it certainly was interesting. And overall, things were going smoothly. I was handling it.

And even managing to make funny stories out of it when we all sat down to dinner that night.

In my calendar that night, before I went to bed, I wrote: *Dog Food Delivered*.

And underneath it, in smaller letters: *Groc Delivered Late*.

Saturday

    Softball and Mother's Day: it's an unbeatable combination. I think this should become a BSC tradition. Or maybe it'll become a Stoneybrook tradition. Whatever happens, the BSC mother-kid softball game was a winning combination!

"A great day for softball," said Kristy, as if she'd ordered up the weather herself.

Stacey adjusted Marnie Barrett's sun hat and moved her stroller a little further back into the shade of the tree at the edge of the bleachers. It was a great day for softball, but a little hot for toddlers.

Even though the game wasn't due to begin for another half hour, the bleachers were already filling up. So was the field of Stoneybrook Elementary School, where we were having the game.

Out on the field, under Kristy's watchful eye, the two teams were warming up, although they hadn't exactly divided into teams yet. It was odd to see parents you were accustomed to seeing in work clothes suddenly transformed into athletes. Mrs. Barrett, for example, who is always immaculately dressed, just like an executive, had on a pair of baggy gray sweat pants, her BSC Mother's Day game T-shirt, and an old St. Louis Cardinals hat pulled down over her forehead. She was thumping her fist in her glove and saying, "Put it here, Buddy. Come on, throw that ball!"

In the outfield, Mrs. Papadakis and Dr. Johanssen were practicing throwing grounders to each other. Mrs. Pike was racing around the bases, laughing.

Some of the kids were warming up, too. But others were standing there with their mouths open.

The motion of something large and pink caught Stacey's eye in the parking lot and she realized that Kristy's grandmother, Nannie, had arrived in her old car, which she has painted pink and which everyone calls the Pink Clinker. Pink is Nannie's favorite color, so it wasn't surprising that she was wearing a pink windbreaker.

As she walked by, Stacey saw that she had written the word "Umpire" in adhesive on her back.

Bart saw her coming, too, and trotted over to shake hands. A moment later, Nannie reached in her pocket and produced a roll of adhesive tape and began to write "umpire" on the back of Bart's black T-shirt.

More people arrived. I had gotten there on time with Maria and Tiffany. I'd been hoping Dad would come, but I sort of knew better. I was playing on the moms' team and Maria was playing on the kids' team. For a moment, I thought about asking Tiffany if she wanted to join the Krushers cheerleaders. But I knew better about that, too.

Claudia was doing a brisk business at the refreshment stand, with Mal's help. "Come on," I said. I took Tiffany over to the stand. "Tiffany, you remember Claudia and Mallory," I said. Tiffany nodded.

"It looks like they need some help here," I began.

"We sure do," said Mallory. "Could you give us a hand, Tiffany?"

Tiffany nodded again. I gave Mallory a "thank-you" look and Maria and I headed for the field.

At least half a dozen proud fathers/husbands were walking around with video cameras, getting all the action live. I wondered what Dad was doing at the office. Too bad he was missing out on the fun.

The Krushers cheerleaders, Vanessa Pike, Haley Braddock, and Charlotte Johanssen, were already leading the crowd in cheers such as: "Hey, hey, take it away/Let's win one for Mother's Day!"

Kristy, who was coaching the kids' team, looked at her watch and blew the whistle loudly. "Kids' team, over here!" she called. She pointed. "Mothers' team, you have the benches over there."

The two teams separated and went to their respective "dugouts."

"Cold drinks, cold drinks," shouted Claudia, walking through the stands holding a small cooler.

The umpires walked to the center of the field. Then Nannie whipped out her whistle and said, "Team captains, please come to the center of the field so we can explain the rules and toss the coin to see who goes first."

The moms conferred furiously for a moment, then Kristy's mom walked out onto the field to face Kristy! The four of them, the two umpires and the two captains, talked for a few minutes, then Bart pulled a quarter out of his pocket and tossed it in the air.

The moms won the toss. Kristy and her mother went back to their respective dugouts and Bart turned to face the stands. "Quiet, please!" he shouted. "I will now explain the rules. They are different from regular softball rules, so please listen carefully — or you won't know when to boo the umpire."

A ripple of laughter went through the stands. Bart said, "This will be a five-inning game. We'll have a third inning stretch . . ." Bart went on, explaining the rest of the rules.

Then Nannie blew her whistle again. "PLAAAAAY BALL!" she shouted.

The moms came out swinging. Mrs. Barrett led off with a single. Kristy's mom followed with another single. Then Dr. Johanssen grounded one to third and Mrs. Barrett got caught in a rundown between second and third base before Matthew Braddock, who was playing third, finally tagged her.

"You'rreeeee out!" cried Nannie, jerking her thumb over her shoulder. Mrs. Barrett trotted off the field to cheers and applause (with especially loud cheering coming from her fiancé, Franklin DeWitt, and his kids) and tipped her hat as she left.

Two runners on base, with one out. Linny Papadakis, who was pitching, wound up and threw a wild pitch. Byron Pike just barely caught it.

"Don't let your mom psych you out!" someone called from the stands.

Mrs. Papadakis tapped her bat against the plate and hunched over again.

Linny threw again. This time the ball was high, but Mrs. Papadakis hit it anyway.

It made a long looping curve toward the outfield — and Claire Pike.

"Claiiiiiiire," bellowed Kristy.

Claire's head jerked up. Her eyes got round. She threw her hand up over her head. Fortunately, it was the hand with the glove on it.

And a miracle occurred. The ball dropped into Claire's glove.

She was so surprised she just stood there with her mouth open.

Kristy's mom tagged up at second and made a run for third.

"Throw to third, throw to third!" Claire's team pleaded.

Suddenly Claire woke up. She grabbed the ball and threw it to Jackie at second. Jackie caught it, spun around, and started to fall down.

A collective groan went up from the crowd.

"SLIDE!" someone screamed in the crowd. It was Watson, Kristy's stepfather. "SLIIIIDE!"

Kristy's mother slid into third base just as the ball Jackie had somehow (miracle #2) managed to throw plopped into Matt's glove.

Bart was there. He swept his hands out. "SAFFFFE!"

When the kids came up to bat, the moms were ahead 3–0.

The kids fought back. With Dr. Johanssen pitching and Kristy's mom catching, Buddy Barrett hit a double. He stayed on second base while Jamie Newton popped out to Mrs. Rodowsky, who was playing first. Then Suzie Barrett got a walk. And Matt Braddock brought Buddy home with another double.

The score at the bottom of the first ended up 3–2, moms' favor.

The crowd went wild.

"Home run, home run!" called the cheerleaders. "Show that kids are number one!"

"I don't believe this," said Jessi, who was taking care of Jamie Newton's baby sister Lucy. She settled Lucy comfortably in her stroller and sat down next to her. "This is amazing."

Marnie had awakened and turned to stare at the sleeping Lucy. "Baby," she said at last.

Stacey and Jessi looked at each other and burst out laughing.

Thanks to a Rodowsky family rally, with Jackie's brother Archie hitting a triple to right field, the game was tied in the second inning.

Mrs. Rodowsky put her hands on her hips and pushed her hat back as the ball sailed through the air. She grinned, then frowned, then shook her head.

"Good hit, Archie," she called. Then she turned to her teammates. "We'll get it back," she told them.

Sitting in the stands, Mr. Papadakis let loose with an amazing cheer, then stood up and tried to get a wave started. In no time at all, the parents and all the spectators were making their own mini-wave, back and forth, in the Stoneybrook Elementary School bleachers.

"This is awesome," Mallory Pike said, coming up beside Stacey and Jessi.

"How's the refreshment stand going?" Jessi asked.

"Claudia and I are selling out. We may have to go get more soda at the third-inning stretch."

Stacey nodded her head with satisfaction. "This will be great for the BSC treasury."

In the third inning, I actually caught a ball hit by Hannie Papadakis. It was a grounder, but I stopped it and kept Hannie from going to second base.

"Yeah, Shannon!" cried an unexpected voice. I looked over to see that Tiffany had inched closer to the field. I grinned and flashed her a victory sign.

A moment later, I heard Tiffany cheer again as Maria hit a solid single and moved Claire Pike from third base to home.

Tie game again. And it stayed that way through the third inning.

"Okay," Kristy told her team as it gathered around her on the bench. "You were down but you've fought back. Keep up the good work." Matt (who is deaf) had been watching Kristy's lips closely. Now he laughed and signed slowly, so that Kristy could understand. She burst out laughing and some of the other kids who could read sign language started laughing, too. Kristy told the other kids what Matt had said: "These moms are killers!"

In the moms' dugout, I listened in amazement as Kristy's mom gave a pep talk that could have been written by Kristy herself. Like mother like daughter, I thought as Mrs. Brewer went through the points of the game. She concluded with, "You know, if we let these kids beat us, we'll never hear the end of it." The moms all put their right hands together and shouted, "Goooo, moms!"

It had turned into a real ball game.

CHAPTER 13

I sat on the team bench and listened to the roar of the crowd. And also some of the talk.

"I used to play intramural sports in college," said Mrs. Barrett. "I'd forgotten how much fun it is, being on a team."

Mrs. Papadakis nodded. "I know. I used to be on a soccer team in high school. It's a great feeling."

Mrs. Rodowsky put two fingers up to her lips and gave a loud whistle.

Mr. Papadakis came over with Sari in his arms. He leaned over and kissed Mrs. Papadakis on the cheek. "You're doing *great*," he told her.

"I bet you say that to all the ball players," teased Mrs. Papadakis.

Mr. Papadakis grinned. "You're all doing great."

Mr. Johanssen reached around the edge of

the dugout and handed Dr. Johanssen a cup of soda. "Thank you," said Dr. Johanssen.

The two Johanssens stood side by side for a moment, watching the game and watching Charlotte cheer. Dr. Johanssen slipped her hand into Mr. Johanssen's as they stood there.

Then she said, turning toward the other players in the dugout, "I'm so glad I got to come today. I'm on call, but other doctors will be handling everything but emergencies for me. Sometimes I can't work it out, but this time, I was determined to."

Mrs. Papadakis said, "I wouldn't have missed it for anything, either. It's the perfect end to a good week. It makes me realize how lucky I am, family, friends . . . now if we just don't lose this game!"

Everyone laughed.

And then it was our turn to go back on the field.

How can I describe that fourth inning? Otherworldly might be a good start. The kids rallied and took the lead. And they held on to it all the way to the fifth.

That's when the moms really got tough.

Mrs. Papadakis hit a double and ran like crazy . . . and slid headfirst into third base.

The crowd went mega-wild, including Hannie and Linny in the outfield.

Mr. Papadakis could be heard cheering in the next county, practically, as Mrs. Papadakis got up and brushed the dirt off her hands.

Dr. Johanssen struck out, and left the plate shaking her head.

Mrs. Rodowsky got to first base on balls.

Then Mrs. Barrett came up. She looked down the third base line. She looked down the first base line. Then she actually pointed her bat down the first base line as if to say, "That's where it's going."

Was she bluffing?

A sudden hush fell over the crowd.

Strike one.

The bat stayed on Mrs. Barrett's shoulder.

The next pitch was a ball.

The next pitch was a "Strike," called Nannie.

And the next pitch — was a screaming line drive down the first-base line.

Mrs. Barrett drove in two easy runs.

The kids had another inning. But they just weren't tough enough to beat their moms. The kids went down one, two three. The game was over. The moms had won, 6–5.

The teams shook hands while the crowds poured onto the field and mobbed the players. The moms and their families actually hoisted Mrs. Barrett up in the air on their shoulders, cheering her. Then they did a cheer for Mrs. Papadakis and then for the whole team.

Then they did a cheer for the kids.

"Hey, moms!" Vanessa Pike shouted. "Thank you for your cheer! Wait till *next* year!"

Gradually the two teams drifted apart and became parts of families again. I overheard snatches of conversations as they went to their cars, or started walking home: "Victory dinner, my treat," I heard Mrs. Papadakis say. Other families laughed and talked and made plans for the night and the next day. Everyone seemed to have such busy, full lives.

We helped Claudia and Mallory pack the refreshment table and leftover refreshments in the back of the Kishis' car. Then Mal ran over to join her family, who was waiting for her in the two Pike family station wagons, crammed with cheering, noisy, cheerful Pikes.

Claudia waved and climbed into the car beside her father and they headed home for dinner.

"I told Nannie we would walk home," said Kristy.

"Great," said Mary Anne, who was sleeping over at Kristy's. "It's such a nice night."

It was, too. The warm day was turning cool as the sun went down. Tiffany, Maria, Mary Anne, Kristy, and I walked slowly down the streets.

Through the windows, I could see people getting ready for dinner, or to go out. Kids were playing basketball with their mothers and fathers using hoops attached to the sides of garages. People were walking dogs together, or finishing up yardwork, or just sitting on porches or steps and talking.

Families. All kinds of families doing all kinds of things.

Together.

Our house was quiet when we returned home. Dad still hadn't gotten back from work, and Mrs. Bryar didn't come on Saturday. I pulled out some leftovers and we made dinner.

Nobody talked much, but it was a peaceful silence, not the tense silence that often fell over us when one or both of our parents were there.

As we finished dinner, I noticed Maria's head nodding.

"Go on to bed," I told her. "I'll clean up in the kitchen. You too, Tiffany."

"Thanks," said Maria and slid off her chair.

I smiled at my reflection in the window over the sink as I rinsed the dishes and loaded them in the dishwasher, remembering how the meter reader had scared me the first day I'd been in charge of the house. Now the week was almost over. In less than forty-eight hours,

Mom would be home. My job as a stand-in mother was done.

It had been a good day, and a good week.

I knew I'd done a good job, too. I wanted to see Mom again, of course, but I was kind of sorry the week had to end.

CHAPTER 14

Sunday morning after breakfast I drifted from room to room, trying to look the house over with a critical eye. Was there anything that needed fixing, straightening, moving, mending? Was I not seeing things that needed doing that my mom would point out the moment she got home tomorrow?

But I couldn't see anything. The house looked good. The dishes had stayed clean, Mrs. Bryar had come on schedule. Even the leftovers were all in neat little containers, with the contents and dates written on labels on top. I'd done some of the grocery shopping and meal planning, but I hadn't had to — Mrs. Bryar could have done it. I'd just wanted to, because it had made me feel like I was in charge.

Like I was useful and doing something.

I'd finished the Sunday paper and left it out for Dad when he got back from the golf course (where else?). I was tired of reading. There was nothing on TV. And with school out, I didn't have any studying to do.

It was too early to call anybody. I wondered what Tiffany and Maria were up to. Tiffany was probably in her garden. Maybe I'd just go out there and . . .

My thoughts came to a screeching halt.

My mom. *This must be what Mom felt like!* This must be why she'd gotten so overly involved in my life.

Because she didn't have anything else to do. The housework was taken care of. Dad was hardly ever around. We were growing up and didn't need her so much anymore. Her job description as a mother had changed. And she didn't have any other job, except running the house.

I remembered all the lists I'd made before I'd taken the job over. I didn't need those lists now. In one week, I'd mastered what I needed to know.

Oh sure, there hadn't been any major disasters. But that was true most of the time. My week had been easy. And fun because the experience was a new one. But now the novelty was wearing off. And it wasn't fun anymore. It wasn't a challenge.

It was just plain boring.

Poor Mom.

Did she think that because we didn't need her the way we had when we were babies that we didn't love her anymore? Or as much? Was that why she kept calling me Shanny and treating me like a baby? Double wow.

In another minute, I'd made a decision. We were going to give Mom a special welcome home party.

I went out to the garden and got Tiffany, who followed with surprisingly little protest. Then I went upstairs and got Maria. I told them my plan.

We decided to make a welcome home dinner from the ground up, instead of using things that Mrs. Bryar had made. We pulled out the cookbooks and flipped through them until we found something we thought we could handle: roast chicken and salad and steamed carrots with parsley butter and mashed potatoes. And a cake. That sounded good and plain to us. After a week of French food, maybe good and plain would sound good to Mom, too.

This time our trip to the grocery store was pretty straightforward — no detours into Twinkieland (although we did get ice cream to go with the cake). We bought just enough for dinner, so we could carry it home on the bus, and not have to wait for a delivery.

(I was learning!)

We decided to start the cake. And to get

everything ready for cooking the dinner to-morrow. Tiffany read the instructions for the cake aloud while Maria and I wrestled with the pots and pans and utensils.

"Place the chicken, breast side down, in a shallow baking dish," Tiffany read.

We pulled open half a dozen drawers. "Which dish is the right shallow baking dish?" asked Maria.

I didn't know the answer. I just knew that we had a very well-supplied kitchen.

"Here's a picture of the chicken in the baking dish!" Tiffany exclaimed. All three of us studied the picture. We finally picked out (I think) the correct baking dish and put it out to use the next day.

We started the cake. We sifted flour and added ingredients and stirred things together.

We got flour and cocoa powder all over everything.

"You should see your face," Maria said, laughing at me. "You look like Shannon the Snowwoman."

"What about you?" I said. "Check it out, Maria. You are *covered* with cocoa powder."

Tiffany said, "Tomorrow we should start the chicken first, then the carrots and the potatoes. The carrots only take twenty minutes. That's not nearly as long as the chicken."

"Good call, Tiffany," I said. "We might have ended up with carrot mush."

At last we got the cake in the oven.

Tiffany made a face. Then she slid off her chair. "I'm going to go get some flowers for the table while the cake bakes," she announced.

"And I'm going to make welcome home decorations," said Maria.

"I'll make a welcome home card," I said.

Soon Maria was hanging up paper chains while Tiffany arranged flowers in a vase to go on the dining room table. I'd just stuck the card in the envelope and put it where Mom would sit and was about to start setting the table when a voice said, "What's all this?"

"Oh, hi, Dad," said Maria. "Mom's coming back tomorrow. We thought we'd surprise her."

"Oh — how nice!"

"Dad!" I pulled Dad out onto the back porch. "You haven't forgotten that Mom's coming back tomorrow, have you?"

Looking indignant, he said, "No, of course not, Shannon."

"We've missed Mom," I said.

Dad nodded. Then he said, "Not that you haven't done a good job, Shannon. I'm proud of the way you took charge."

I shook my head. "It wasn't that hard. The house practically runs itself, especially with Mrs. Bryar taking care of it."

I drew in a deep breath. Should I tell my father what I'd figured out? How much would he understand? Crossing my fingers for luck, I went on, "In fact, I think I sort of understand why Mom seems so, well, lonely."

I let my voice trail off as a look of pain — or possibly guilt — flashed across my father's face.

"I know," he said, as much to himself as to me. "I know."

We sat in silence for a moment. Then Dad reached over and patted my knee. "You did a good job," he said again. "I'm proud of you. Of all of you. My girls."

He jumped up and cleared his throat. "Now. What about going out for dinner? Maybe the Chinese restaurant. Would you girls like that?"

"Super!" I said.

Dad laughed and stood up. "Let me go change out of my golf clothes. And you guys better, uh, wash some of that cooking you've been doing off your faces."

Ooops! I'd forgotten about the flour.

I went back inside and told Maria and Tiffany we were going out for dinner.

We finished decorating the dining room and

took the cake out of the oven and set it out to cool.

As I washed the flour off my face, and went back downstairs to join my family, I wondered if it was possible that my family — and my mother and father — cared more about each other than I realized? That they'd just gotten locked into patterns that kept them from saying so, from showing it?

And if that was what had happened, maybe it wasn't too late to change.

Feeling suddenly hopeful, I went outside and sat on the front step. The smell of the cake still filled the air. Upstairs, I could hear, faintly, Dad's footsteps as he moved around, the sound of water running as Maria washed cocoa powder off her face.

A person looking through the window of our house would see a family, like other families, getting ready for dinner, getting ready for the evening, getting ready for jobs and family activities and the work of the evening and the next day.

Maybe it was possible that what they were seeing wasn't such an illusion after all.

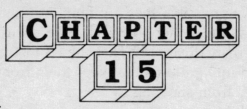

CHAPTER 15

Mom would be home in the late afternoon.

Maria and Tiffany and I finished decorating the dining room. We set the table. Tiffany added fresh flowers to the arrangement she'd started the day before.

We started the chicken right after lunch. Mrs. Bryan confirmed that we had chosen the right roasting pan and complimented us on our chocolate cake (even though it had fallen a bit in the middle). Then she helped us make cream cheese frosting.

Dad had said the night before that he would get home early, but I hadn't seen him that morning. He'd already left for work when I woke up. I was pretty sure he'd forget until the last minute, and that he'd be late. And I was pretty sure it would make Mom feel bad.

But at least she had a surprise party waiting for her.

As it turned out, I had a surprise, too.

Dad came home early.

"Dad?" I said. I couldn't believe my eyes.

"Shannon?" Dad teased. "I wanted to make sure we're on time to meet your mom."

The four of us piled into the car and took off for the airport.

Dad hummed under his breath as he drove. And we were a whole half hour early. With Dad still humming, he headed for the gate area where Mom would be arriving.

Suddenly Dad said, "You girls wait right here."

He sprinted away. A business call he'd forgotten to make? I wondered. But he'd left his briefcase.

The puzzle was solved a few minutes later when Dad came sprinting back, carrying a bouquet of red roses. He must have gotten them at one of the airport flower stands.

They weren't as pretty as Tiffany's flowers, I thought. But I knew my mom would think they were beautiful.

I was right. Mom walked into the waiting area and stopped, looking around. For a moment, I could see her as a person and not only our mom. For a moment, I saw how confident she could look, how smart and together.

Then she saw us and smiled and we all rushed forward to hug each other.

"It was wonderful, it was wonderful," Mom

kept saying. "But it's so good to be home!"

She saw the roses then, and was suddenly quiet. "For me?" she said at last.

My father made an embarrassed gesture. "They're just, you know, from the flower stand."

"They're perfect," said my mom and she flung her arms around Dad.

"Shannon!" Greer came running toward me. Her week in Paris hadn't changed her much, except she was wearing a beret at an impossible angle on the side of her head, and a little more makeup than usual.

"Bonjour!" I cried, hugging her. "How was it?"

"Incredible! *Fantastique*. We've decided the French class is going again next year, and *this* time, you're coming, too!"

Polly burst in, "And guess what — we each bought you the most outrageous, silliest souvenir we could think of. Mine's a wind-up Eiffel Tower that plays the French National Anthem, and it hops! You've got to see it. It's in my luggage."

"You didn't forget my French chocolates, did you?" I asked in mock horror.

"Of course not. Although the food on the plane was so awful — "

I grinned. I'd hear all about it tomorrow.

But for right now, it was good to see my friends again, and to hear them talk.

I turned back to my family. My father was grinning and my mother was wearing a grin to match. Both Tiffany and Maria were looking surprised. And a little dazed.

"So," my father said. "What do you think? I've rescheduled my trip and I'll leave in a couple of days. I want to go home and be part of your . . ."

I made a face at Dad. He was about to give away Mom's homecoming surprise party.

But he caught himself at the last minute. ". . . a part of your homecoming," he concluded.

"That's great, Dad," I said.

Together we all walked out of the airport and headed for home.

If you'd looked through the window of our house that night, you'd have seen a family gathered around a dinner table, beneath homemade decorations, with a vase of roses on the sideboard and a gathering of garden flowers as a centerpiece. You would have seen candles lit in silver holders and a lopsided chicken being carved into lopsided pieces and served around the table. You wouldn't have been able to tell that the carrots were a little mushy, or that the potatoes were sort of salty.

You would have thought we were the perfect family.

And you would have been wrong.

Dad and Mom were formal at first, after that early excitement of seeing each other and realizing (I think) that they'd missed each other. They were awkward and careful, as if they'd been hurt and didn't want to take that chance again. But the old tension that had made other family dinners so difficult was hardly there at all. Both of them were trying very hard.

And Mom still said things that drove me crazy, such as, "Shanny, you really don't need to wear so much makeup, you know."

To which I answered, "Okay, Mom."

It wasn't the greatest answer in the world, and it didn't solve any problems. But at least it didn't start a new one.

Maria jumped up and got the cake. She cut everybody big, ragged pieces and Tiffany and I scooped out ice cream and placed it strategically to hide the worse places in the cake.

It tasted pretty good.

Mom said it was the best cake she'd ever had.

Summer was getting properly started now. BSC business was slow, but I still had enough work to keep me in mall money. Maria was spending a good bit of time keeping in shape for swimming — and talking about her new interest: the Iron Man Triathalon. Tiffany was putting new plants into her garden and looking satisfied and keeping us supplied with flowers and new lettuce.

Dad had left on his trip and sent back a postcard, which we'd stuck on the refrigerator along with the card from Paris that Mom had sent us (it arrived the day *after* she did).

And one morning, as I was sitting at the kitchen table, not doing much of anything at all, Mom sat down by me with her cup of coffee.

"You really did do a good job, honey," she said.

"Thanks."

"I was sorry you didn't go on the trip, but maybe this time apart has been good for both of us," Mom went on.

"I think so," I said cautiously.

Mom laced her fingers around her coffee cup and took a sip. "I guess we've needed to talk for a long time."

"I guess so," I said.

Looking up, Mom smiled a little. "We used to be close. How did things change so much? When?"

"I think," I said, choosing my words carefully, "it was when I began growing up. . . .

Mom, it's not that I don't love you. I do. But you're just too *involved* in all our lives, especially mine. I mean, I still need you to be my mother, but I am growing up and I . . . I have my own life. Separate."

"I see," said Mom.

"So what I was thinking," I rushed on, "was maybe if you had a job, you wouldn't need to be involved in our lives so much." Get a life, Mom. That's what I was saying. Only I didn't mean it in the harsh way that sounded.

To my amazement, Mom said, "You're right."

She went on, "While I was in Paris, I got to know the other chaperones a bit. Two of them have jobs outside their houses. They were a lot of fun to get to know — competent, involved. It made me remember when I used to be like that. I don't know when it happened, but somehow, I lost that. I'd like to get it back. Get *me* back."

"Wow. That's great, Mom." I paused, then added, "Some trip, huh?"

"Some trip," Mom agreed.

The phone rang and Mom reached over to pick it up. "Oh, hi! My daughter Shannon and I were just talking about you. I told her about meeting you and how you inspired me to start on my next career. . . . Well, no, not yet. . . .

Lunch? This Friday? And you'll help me to
. . . oh, that's great. . . ."

I smiled and slipped out of the kitchen.
We'd both made a trip of sorts. Away from
each other in some ways. Back toward each
other in new ways.

Maybe our family could become a real family
again.

Who knew?

In a way, the trip was only just beginning.

About the Author

ANN M. MARTIN did *a lot* of baby-sitting when she was growing up in Princeton, New Jersey. She is a former editor of books for children, and was graduated from Smith College.

Ms. Martin lives in New York City with her cats, Mouse and Rosie. She likes ice cream and *I Love Lucy*; and she hates to cook.

Ann Martin's Apple Paperbacks include *Yours Turly, Shirley*; *Ten Kids, No Pets*; *With You and Without You*; *Bummer Summer*; and all the other books in the Baby-sitters Club series.

by Ann M. Martin

More titles... ▶

The Baby-sitters Club titles continued...

☐ MG45659-8	#58 Stacey's Choice	$3.50
☐ MG45660-1	#59 Mallory Hates Boys (and Gym)	$3.50
☐ MG45662-8	#60 Mary Anne's Makeover	$3.50
☐ MG45663-6	#61 Jessi's and the Awful Secret	$3.50
☐ MG45664-4	#62 Kristy and the Worst Kid Ever	$3.50
☐ MG45665-2	#63 Claudia's Freind Friend	$3.50
☐ MG45666-0	#64 Dawn's Family Feud	$3.50
☐ MG45667-9	#65 Stacey's Big Crush	$3.50
☐ MG47004-3	#66 Maid Mary Anne	$3.50
☐ MG47005-1	#67 Dawn's Big Move	$3.50
☐ MG47006-X	#68 Jessi and the Bad Baby-Sitter	$3.50
☐ MG47007-8	#69 Get Well Soon, Mallory!	$3.50
☐ MG47008-6	#70 Stacey and the Cheerleaders	$3.50
☐ MG47009-4	#71 Claudia and the Perfect Boy	$3.50
☐ MG47010-8	#72 Dawn and the We Love Kids Club	$3.50
☐ MG45575-3	Logan's Story Special Edition Readers' Request	$3.25
☐ MG47118-X	Logan Bruno, Boy Baby-sitter Special Edition Readers' Request	$3.50
☐ MG44240-6	Baby-sitters on Board! Super Special #1	$3.95
☐ MG44239-2	Baby-sitters' Summer Vacation Super Special #2	$3.95
☐ MG43973-1	Baby-sitters' Winter Vacation Super Special #3	$3.95
☐ MG42493-9	Baby-sitters' Island Adventure Super Special #4	$3.95
☐ MG43575-2	California Girls! Super Special #5	$3.95
☐ MG43576-0	New York, New York! Super Special #6	$3.95
☐ MG44963-X	Snowbound Super Special #7	$3.95
☐ MG44962-X	Baby-sitters at Shadow Lake Super Special #8	$3.95
☐ MG45661-X	Starring the Baby-sitters Club Super Special #9	$3.95
☐ MG45674-1	Sea City, Here We Come! Super Special #10	$3.95

Available wherever you buy books...or use this order form.

Scholastic Inc., P.O. Box 7502, 2931 E. McCarty Street, Jefferson City, MO 65102

Please send me the books I have checked above. I am enclosing $_____ (please add $2.00 to cover shipping and handling). Send check or money order - no cash or C.O.D.s please.

Name _____ Birthdate_____

Address _____

City_____ State/Zip _____

Please allow four to six weeks for delivery. Offer good in the U.S. only. Sorry, mail orders are not available to residents of Canada. Prices subject to change.

BSC993

THE **BIGGEST** BSC SWEEPSTAKES EVER!

Scholastic and Ann M. Martin want to thank all of the Baby-sitters Club fans for a cool 100 million books in print! Celebrate by sending in your entry now!

ENTER AND YOU CAN WIN:

• *10 Grand Prizes:* Win one of ten $2,500 prizes!
Your cash prize is good towards any artistic, academic, or sports pursuit. Take a dance workshop, go to soccer camp, get a violin tutor, learn a foreign language! You decide and Scholastic will pay the expense up to $2,500 value. Sponsored by Scholastic Inc., the Ann M. Martin Foundation, Kid Vision, Milton Bradley® and Kenner® Products.

• *100 First Prizes:* Win one of 100 fabulous runner-up gifts selected for you by Scholastic including a limited supply of BSC videos, autographed limited editions of Ann Martin's upcoming holiday book, T-shirts, board games and other fabulous merchandise!

Just fill in the coupon below or write the information on a 3" x 5" piece of paper and mail to: **THE BSC REMEMBERS SWEEPSTAKES,** Scholastic Inc., P.O. Box 7500, 2931 East McCarty Street, Jefferson City, MO 65102. Entries must be postmarked by 10/31/94.

Send to Scholastic Inc., P.O. Box 7500, 2931 East McCarty Street, Jefferson City, MO 65102.

THE BSC REMEMBERS SWEEPSTAKES

Name _____   Birthdate _____

Address _____   Phone# _____

City _____   State _____ Zip _____

Where did you buy this book?   ❑ Bookstore   ❑ Other(Specify)

Name of Bookstore _____

BSCR194

ENTER SCHOLASTIC'S

THE BSC REMEMBERS SWEEPSTAKES

Official Rules:

No purchase necessary. To enter use the official entry form or a 3" x 5" piece of paper and hand print your full name, complete address, day telephone number and birthdate. Enter as often as you wish, one entry to an envelope. Mechanically reproduced entries are void. Mail to THE BSC REMEMBERS Sweepstakes at the address provided on the previous page, postmarked by 10/31/94. Scholastic Inc. is not responsible for late, lost or postage due mail. Sweepstakes open to residents of the U.S.A. 6-15 years old upon entering. Employees of Scholastic Inc., Kid Vision, Milton Bradley Inc., Kenner Inc., Ann M. Martin Foundation, their affiliates, subsidiaries, dealers, distributors, printers, mailers, and their immediate families are ineligible. Prize winners will be randomly drawn from all eligible entries under the supervision of Smiley Promotion Inc., an independent judging organization whose decisions are final. Prizes: Ten Grand Prizes each $2,500 awarded toward any artistic, academic or sports pursuit approved by Scholastic Inc. Winner may also choose $2,500 cash payment. An approved pursuit costing less than $2,500 must be verified by bona fide invoice and presented to Scholastic Inc. prior to 7/31/95 to receive the cash difference. One hundred First Prizes each a selection by Scholastic Inc. of BSC videos, Ann Martin books, t-shirts and games. Estimated value each $10.00. Sweepstakes void where prohibited, subject to all federal, state, provincial, local laws and regulations. Odds of winning depend on the number of entries received. Prize winners are notified by mail. Grand Prize winners and parent/legal guardian are mailed a Affidavit of Eligibility/ Liability/ Publicity/Release to be executed and returned within 14 days of its date or an alternate winner may be drawn. Only one prize allowed a person or household. Taxes on prize, expenses incurred outside of prize provision and any injury, loss or damages incurred by acceptance and use of prizes are the sole responsibility of the winners and their parent/legal guardian. Prizes cannot be exchanged, transferred or cashed. Scholastic Inc. reserves the right to substitute prizes of like value if any offered are unavailable and to use the names and likenesses of prize winners without further compensation for advertising and promotional use. Prizes that are unclaimed or undelivered to winner's address remain the property of Scholastic Inc. For a Winners List, please send a stamped, addressed envelope to THE BSC REMEMBERS Sweepstakes Winners, Smiley Promotion Inc., 271 Madison Avenue, #802, New York, N.Y. 10016 after 11/30/94. Residents of Washington state may omit return stamp.

Celebrate the Holiday with

Secret Santa
by Ann M. Martin

It's Christmastime, and the Baby-sitters are
holding a Secret Santa drawing.
Each Club member puts one wish in a hat,
and then draws someone else's wish to
grant. You'll have to open their mail to
discover how this special holiday turns
out — and how the BSC members make one
little girl's Christmas the best ever!

**Real
cards, letters,
and friendship
necklaces
for you
and a
friend!**

If you loved *The Baby-sitters Club Chain Letter,*
you'll love this perfect holiday gift for all BSC fans!

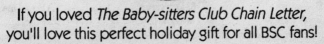

Don't miss out on
The All New

BABY-SITTERS®
Fan Club

Join now!
Your one-year membership package includes:

- The exclusive Fan Club T-Shirt!
- A Baby-sitters Club poster!
- A Baby-sitters Club note pad and pencil!
- An official membership card!
- The exclusive *Guide to Stoneybrook!*

Plus four additional newsletters per year

so you can be the first to know the hot news about the series — Super Specials, Mysteries, Videos, and more — the baby-sitters, Ann Martin, and lots of baby-sitting fun from the Baby-sitters Club Headquarters!

ALL THIS FOR JUST $6.95 plus $1.00 postage and handling! **You can't get all this great stuff anywhere else except THE BABY-SITTERS FAN CLUB!**

Just fill in the coupon below and mail with payment to: THE BABY-SITTERS FAN CLUB, Scholastic Inc., P.O. Box 7500, 2931 E. McCarty Street, Jefferson City, MO 65102.

THE BABY-SITTERS FAN CLUB

___ YES! Enroll me in The Baby-sitters Fan Club! I've enclosed my check or money order (no cash please) for $7.95

Name _____ Birthdate _____

Street _____

City _____ State/Zip _____

Where did you buy this book?

❑ Bookstore   ❑ Drugstore   ❑ Supermarket
❑ Book Fair   ❑ Book Club   ❑ other_____

BSFC593

Create Your Own Mystery Stories!

MYSTERY GAME!

WHO: Boyfriend   **WHY:** Romance

WHAT: Phone Call   **WHERE:** Dance

Use the special Mystery Case card to pick WHO did it, WHAT was involved, WHY it happened and WHERE it happened. Then dial secret words on your Mystery Wheels to add to the story! Travel around the special Stoneybrook map gameboard to uncover your friends' secret word clues! Finish four baby-sitting jobs and find out all the words to win. Then have everyone join in to tell the story!

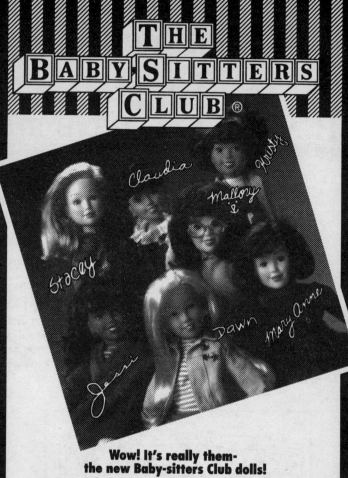

Wow! It's really them—
the new Baby-sitters Club dolls!

Your favorite Baby-sitters Club characters have come to life in these
beautiful collector dolls. Each doll wears her own unique clothes and jewelry.
They look just like the girls you have imagined! The dolls also come with their own
individual stories in special edition booklets that you'll find nowhere else.

Look for the new Baby-sitters Club collection...
coming soon to a store near you!

Kenner®